TALL TALES

AND

Short Stories

from SOUTH JERSEY

Edited by Amy Hollinger and Marie Gilbert

ISBN-13: 978-1478106197
ISBN-10: 1478106190

This collection is respectfully dedicated to the local businesses that have provided meeting space (and caffeine!) to the South Jersey Writers' Group over the past several years. Thanks for your support of local writers!

Quarter Note Café
And the Conservatory of Musical Arts
57 East Kings Highway
Audubon, NJ

Treehouse Coffee Shop
120 West Merchant Street
Audubon, NJ

Jersey Java & Tea
140 N. Haddon Ave
Haddonfield, NJ

Wegmans Market Cafe
2100 Route 70 West
Cherry Hill, NJ

The South Jersey Writers' Group meets regularly for topic-based discussion about writing and the publishing process. For our calendar of events and membership options, visit www.meetup.com/south-jersey-writers.

TABLE OF CONTENTS

THE PHILLY GIRL IN JERSEY

Joanne Costantino

I never wanted to move to New Jersey. I was born and raised in Philly. In my mind, Jersey was a Sunday drive to visit the "Jersey cousins." The attraction for me, as a city kid, was that each of my Jersey cousins had a pool and a large back yard, with grass and trees. We had a backyard too, but it was about the size of a cemetery plot, and required not much attention. Just big enough to grow a few tomato plants in buckets. Trees in Philly were only found in parks. Even so, I always thought that New Jersey was a nice place to visit, but I wouldn't want to live there.

There was no public transportation in Jersey. If you wanted go somewhere, you needed someone to drive you if it was too far to walk, and it seemed everywhere was too far to walk.

I'm a girl from the "Northeast" in Philadelphia. I married a guy from South Philly, a section of the city I only understood by way of the maps on the walls of the SEPTA trains indicating stops beyond City Hall. When I first met Mike, he asked me what kind of car I drove. When I told him I didn't have a car, I found out that he and most of his family felt that public transportation was "beneath" them; as if it was something "other"' people of a lesser social status are saddled with.

After we married and had our two daughters, we bought a tiny row house in the Kensington section of the city, exactly two blocks from the Frankford El. It wasn't a perfect neighborhood, but it was the practical choice for that time in our lives as very young newlyweds.

9

My job was in Center City. I needed no car of my own. I took the Frankford El to 8th and Market, walked off the train, through a turnstile and into the building where I worked. I never had to set foot outside if I didn't want to, a real bonus in lousy weather. I could grocery shop at the Reading Terminal Market; I could catch a show after work with friends from work for a night out. I could buy lunch and a huge fruit salad from the street vendors and not even spend five bucks. I could run to City Hall on my lunch break if we needed something official like the official stuff that one gets done at City Hall. It was easy and convenient.

But after thirteen years in Kensington, my husband Mike announced that he wanted to move to New Jersey, and that he had made an appointment to look at a house that seemed to fit our price range.

"We're looking at a house in Jersey on Saturday," he said.

"I have plans to go down the shore with Susan," I said.

"You just go to the shore. I'll take the kids. I'm only looking," he said.

I sighed, and repeated my concerns about a move so far from my parents and the huge change of scenery for the kids. Our daughters were just starting their teenage years, preparing for high school; it would such be a big change. He was not thinking this through.

Katie and Chrissie were well-rounded city kids. The girls were street-savvy and confident when traveling just about any-where, with or without me. They knew how to navigate their way around the city by train or bus as well as on bicycle. Some-times, on weekends, we would get on our bikes and ride to the Delaware River along the old factory and warehouse roads and take rest stops at some of the abandoned docks.

Sometimes those bike rides would take us all the way to South Street. We'd stop for water ice and window shop the storefronts with some of the oddest merchandise, taking turns watching the bikes. It was fun for all of us.

I was sure that *my* street-savvy, city-dwelling children would find the house-hunting jaunt to New Jersey appalling and unfathomable. They had an appreciation for the outdoors in a natural setting because we were summertime weekend campers, mostly at Jersey campgrounds. It was nice to visit on weekends and to get the kids out of the city for a break in their routines.

But I knew they liked returning to our city home so much that they'd not even consider moving to such a rustic and barbaric setting, sparse of public transportation and no such thing as South Street. Certainly they would see the error of their Dad's thinking and put on such an emotional uproar that he would just stop this silliness.

With that confidence in my offspring, I went my merry way on my day trip down to the Jersey shore while my family kept their date with the Real Estate agent.

When I told my girlfriend Susan, she thought I might be missing out on the house hunt with Mike and the kids. Susan already lived in Jersey, another Northeast girl married to a South Philly guy. She and I had been childhood friends, through high school and since; our husbands' friendship went back even further. Susan had wanted to move to Jersey. She was used to driving everywhere she went, and was never fond of public transportation.

I assured her that I had no intention of relocating to South Jersey and neither did my kids. "It's not that bad," she tried to convince me, going on about all the great places there were to shop and the many movie theaters to choose from and how nice it was to have some land. I knew all that, we traveled with her and her husband, Anthony, on a regular basis. Come to think of it, we were the ones who hiked over to Jersey to do those things with them. Trying to not sound petulant, I responded, "Well, he can look all he wants. I am *not* moving to New Jersey."

Unfortunately for me, my street-savvy, city-dwelling children found the house in New Jersey much more to their liking than I could have imagined. I was betrayed. They had been seduced by a three-quarter acre backyard blanketed in green grass and trees! "Trees, Mom, there's lots of big trees! And room for a pool! And a driveway, with a *garage*!"

That was almost 25 years ago. This Philly girl was dragged, kicking and screaming, to live in Jersey. It is the main chapter of the life I didn't sign up for.

Life is what happens when you tell the universe your plans and the universe says in response, "I don't think so." It's a tweak to your nose that you had better get with the program. Whatever that program might be.

We moved to New Jersey that summer of 1988 and Mike promised that if I gave it at least a year, and was still hellbent on moving back to Philly, we would. As it turned out, fate led me on a direct drive down a Jersey back road to the street of our weekend traveling friends Anthony and Susan. Being so close to them was the main stabilizer for making life in New Jersey somewhat palatable. We spent even more of our weekend time with them (and their pool). Our summer weekends were like a family gathering. It was comfortable.

Fast forward, life happens. Our daughters graduate high school, go to college, meet their future husbands, a wedding, a grand baby, a couple of job changes and I got the news that our friends were relocating south to Virginia. They were moving for a job opportunity. Soon after our farewells, I asked my husband if we could move now.

He was surprised. "You really still don't like it here?"

I guess I had been too compliant and passive those last ten years. I've since lost that character flaw.

He continued, "What about the kids?"

"The kids are grown," I responded.

"But now we have a grandchild," he whined. No, really, he actually whined.

That next year was an emotionally draining one, and the most life-altering in the course of events. My father died shortly after a cancer diagnosis. Soon after, grandbaby number two was born and became brain-damaged. With a need for extra family support and therapy, the new grandbaby and his Mom, Chrissie, moved back home within two months of his birth.

In addition, my mom's health was such that she was unable to live alone, especially in her three-story Victorian house in Philly. She moved in with us, and our briefly empty nest became too crowded for multiple generations. So we traded up to a bigger house, with an in-law suite, in-ground pool, oversized grassy lawn, and even an extra bedroom that I unsuccessfully tried to turn into a Mom cave.

But within two months of settling in, Mom died, and suddenly we had a lot of extra space. More twists and turns and more changes in the life we didn't sign up for soon affirmed my mantra that fate puts you were you are needed, whether or not you planned it.

Soon after, my niece Bridget found herself overwhelmed and somewhat alone as a single mom, trying to work full time and continue her education. Her parents were both too far away from her job and school, but she needed an extended support system. Since Bridget and her sister Theresa were thick as thieves with Katie and Chrissie, even as young adults, Mike and I decided to offer her the extra space. "Six months," she promised. "Six months, tops." "OK," I reassured her, halfheartedly.

The short-lived semi-empty nest was now full up with two toddler boys and their moms. It was busy and noisy and the days flew by. I was often asked by friends why my niece couldn't live with either of her own parents and since it was really none of their business, I would shrug and say, "It doesn't matter, besides, it's what we do."

Once, when it was clear we were well beyond six months, I suggested that Bridget get her driver's license renewed for New Jersey, since that's where she'd landed for the time being.

"Why would I do that?" she asked, looking at me like I was suggesting she cut off a limb.

"Well, you're here for now at least, and probably a little longer. It just seems the practical thing to do until you finish your degree."

"But I have a Pennsylvania license."

"But you live in New Jersey now," I said matter-of-factly.

On the day she did transfer all her vital information to a New Jersey residence she actually said, with almost defeated resignation, "I guess I really am a Jersey girl now. My driver's license says so." Join the club, honey, I didn't plan this either.

Two years after Bridget and her son Sean moved in, daughter Chrissie became engaged, got married and moved out to begin a new family life. The four of us remaining were comfortable and complacent with the way things were for about two more years.

During that time, Bridget's sister Theresa also became a Jersey Girl, buying a condo not more than a mile from our house. Theresa embraced her Jersey girl status with much less mournful resignation than her sister, getting a job in Jersey and earning her Masters degree at a South Jersey college. She even married a Jersey Boy, nicknamed "Goon." (And yes, it suits him, but we love him.)

And Bridget and Theresa's younger sister Lindsay also officially became a Jersey Girl, after commuting from Hatfield, PA to spend every weekend with her boyfriend Alex. Living in New Jersey seven days a week did not hold the same charm, but having her boyfriend and two sisters close by helped. She eventually married him--and also eventually found more things to like than not like about living in Jersey.

Bridget became engaged and moved out with her fiancé to neighboring Mantua. We thought we were finally at the point in our lives when the troop of kids seemed to have their own courses charted, their own home bases. We made plans to downsize, and so put the big house on the market and found a townhouse in Mullica Hill. I did try valiantly to shop the Philadelphia real estate market, but to no avail. Mike is a Jersey Boy now. But I like Mullica Hill. It's artsy and somewhat unpretentious. I could see me living in Mullica Hill. But the universe had other plans again.

The downsizing idea was snuffed by the crashing real estate market and a serious need for my oldest granddaughter to attend a better school system. That's right, we are full up again in a multi-generation household with my eldest daughter Kate, her husband Scot, and their two daughters, Tayler the Timid Teenager and Meghan, aka Todzilla the Tyrant. The thoughts of living through teenage years again don't make me shudder half as much as life with Todzilla; she's six but the name aptly applies, in most situations.

So here I am, still a Philly girl but living a Jersey life. There are things I like about living in New Jersey. I like my grassy lawn and appreciate it even more as long as I can afford to pay someone else to maintain it. I like having a driveway and not having to jockey for a parking space after a long day at work. I like that a lot. I like the big swimming pool in my own backyard. I like the schools. I like my neighbors and as it turns out, most of them are Philly transplants. I like shopping for fresh produce at a Jersey farm. I like being able to watch shooting stars from my back yard in the middle of the night. It's a free show from the universe and a gentle reminder that it can be really nice.

There are some things I will always miss since not living in the city. I miss people walking with a purpose other than exercise or walking the dog. No one walks from his house to the store like WaWa or Starbucks. There is a sports field complex within my development where ball games are played. Folks who live within our development still drive to that field! It can't be the distance, because there isn't a road that's a mile long within our development. Yet they will walk or jog the development for exercise but drive to watch their kid play soccer.

I miss the corner stores. Like the corner grocery store where as you walked in the door, you could smell barrel pickles and that had four foot counter squeezed in a corner to buy lunch meat or hoagies. Although there are hardly any around anymore, I miss the corner luncheonette that made only burgers and cheese steaks, but always had a case full of Breyer's ice cream that could be scooped into cones.

I miss the corner bar. Not any corner bar, but a corner bar that you can walk to and the bartender knows what you'll probably have to drink and has it half poured as hellos are exchanged and "howYOOdooin's?" The corner bar, where half the patrons know something personal about you and your family and that's okay with you. You can walk there, and walk back home. The corner bar that has a wood shuffleboard table, with a well-polished shellac surface and just enough wax dust sprinkled to make those metal quoits glide so silent down to the end of the board that the only sound is a light "clack" on another puck. The corner bar that would offer to sponsor your softball team for the season, not just because of the business generated after the games. Well, that probably had *something* to do with it, but it really was a neighborly and community gesture that reinforced a sense of belonging to our community, an identity as neighbors and friends. I miss the corner bar a lot, especially in the summer. It's the meeting with no agenda needed.

From the looks of the family that has settled in and around me in New Jersey, this is where I'll be for as long as the universe allows. With the grown kids and their kids we have quite a comfortable network of family connected by our initial relocation of home base. I have become the accidental Matriarch of this collection of New Jerseyites. I never planned it. It just seemed to work out that way.

It's not perfect. In fact, there are days when I deliberately stay later at work so I don't have to hear the noise that is my home life, a life I claim I didn't sign up for. The reward comes with little unexpected gestures, like after a particularly bad day, the teenager who "hates her life," puts her head on my shoulder as she passes by me and says, "I love you, Grammy." Or once in a while even Todzilla comes through for me and squeaks out, "You're the bessstt." It's not perfect, but it's what we do and who we are, and it's in New Jersey.

DESTINY IN DUSTY SPRING FIELD

Joseph E. Arechavala

Malaria Pete rode into the town of Dusty Spring Field on his trusty, three-legged Shetland pony named Catsup—"Not Ketchup!" Pete would always say. Nobody knew why either one was named the way they were, but everyone knew both names were really stupid. Pete was short, less than five feet, and his five-gallon hat was a mite too big for his four-gallon head. Only reason his head was four gallons in the first place was because he was such a blowhard.

His keen brown eyes roved up and down the street, expecting trouble but not finding any. He always said the reason he'd lived so long was he was always on the lookout for danger. The real reason was he was so stinking short everybody missed him when they shot. Which they inevitably did because he was so damned annoying.

He rode over to the saloon, Brittney's Place, and tied up his pony. He sauntered in and stood at the bar for ten minutes. When nobody noticed him, he hollered, "Hey! Barkeep! Down here! Gimme a whiskey."

The barkeep leaned over the bar until he saw Pete. "Whoops, didn't see ya standin' there, stranger. Whiskey'll be a nickel."

Pete reached into the pocket of his dungarees and flipped the coin onto the bar with practiced nonchalance. He never reached the counter in any bar he was ever in.

"What's your name, stranger?" a friendly deputy at the bar asked as the bartender handed the shot glass down to Pete.

"Malaria Pete," he replied, and a man sitting at the table across the way immediately jumped up with a yell as he threw his chair across the room; the barmaid ducked out of the way in the nick of time. The piano player stopped playing, waiting for the shooting to begin. He liked a good shootout; it usually gave him a nice long break.

"Malaria Pete?" the man exclaimed, obviously drunk as a skunk as he leaned over to one side. "You killed my sister-in-law's brother's second cousin! Twice-removed! Shot 'im dead from a hundred yards away! Now, I'm gonna git my revenge!"

"Shot a lot of men," Pete answered with indifference. "Where 'bouts this happen?"

"Town of Muddy Puddle!"

"Never been there," Pete stated.

The man's face took on a confused expression. "Huh? Whaddaya mean ya never been there?"

"I ain't never been to Muddy Puddle," Pete repeated with some exasperation. "You sure you're not thinkin' 'bout Cholera Pete? People get us two confused all the time."

The man scratched his head as he considered this new information. "Huh. Guess it wasn't you after all. Sorry 'bout that." He put his hands on his hips. "You know, I'm gittin' old and my memory ain't what it used to be."

"Don't take no offense, my good man," Pete answered good-naturedly. "Happens so often I'm used to it. Suppose it happens to the other Pete, too." Pete waved his hand in forgiveness, and the man lurched back to retrieve his seat as the piano resumed its off-key blaring. Piano player wasn't all that bad actually, but the damned piano couldn't hold a tune for more than two seconds.

The deputy, put off by the incident triggered by his first question, turned his back to Pete and feigned deafness. Next to him, a burly young man named Sebastian—likely the dumbest living creature in the whole territory, including the cows—wasn't put off in the least. "So, what brings ya to town, Mister Malaria Pete?"

"Got a job," Pete replied. "Lookin' for a Mr. Antonio Scruggs after I wet my whistle. Know where I can find 'im?"

"He's in his store down the street a ways. Don't mind if I asks what kinda job is it, Mister Pete, do ya?"

"Not at all. I'm here to kill a man named Bryce Barnes."

The entire bar instantly grew silent.

Another break for the piano player. This was pleasant—two in one day.

The crowd remained silent as Pete downed the shot glass of liquor, flicked it up onto the counter with practiced ease, and left for Scruggs' store. No sooner had the swinging doors clattered behind him than he heard a sound and whirled, guns at the ready.

He stopped in jaw-dropping surprise, for before him stood the one woman who had gotten away from him—Belle McBell, daughter of his late mentor, Liberty.

Liberty McBell had taught Pete everything he'd ever learned about gunfighting, Pete coming to him as a young runaway from the circus. Liberty took him under his protective wing, and the two grew close. Liberty came to think of Pete as his own son, although Pete's dim brain didn't quite get the idea, and he merely considered Liberty as a kind, friendly neighbor.

Liberty had been gone nearly ten years now, dying shortly after being shot – by Pete. The dispute that ended Liberty's life was over Belle. He'd wanted someone a little taller for his darling Amazonian girl of six feet six, and Pete just didn't fill the bill. They argued, and then finally pulled out their guns. Liberty missed, making the same fatal mistake everyone else did. His bullet whizzed a good foot over Pete's head. But Pete's found its mark. Pete's worst fear was confirmed when, after a whole hour came and went, Liberty lay unmoving. He went off to pay his respects to the girl he loved, but knew he'd never have.

Now she stood before him in all her towering glory, gazing down at him with those blue, tender, love blossom eyes.

"Hello, Pete," she quietly said with a smile.

"Why, B-Belle." Pete looked up—and up. His hat fell off. "He-hello. You, uh, livin' here in Dusty Spring Field now?"

"Yes," she replied as she looked down, "I'm—married now, Pete, to a man named Bryce Barnes."

"Barnes? You're married to Barnes?"

19

"Yes, Pete, that's why I had ta come 'n see ya," she answered as the tears began falling down her cheeks, a surging spring waterfall. "I know why you're here, Pete. Please, I'm beggin' ya, don't kill my husband. Please."

All Pete could do was back away in shock. Belle married? And to the man he was supposed to kill? He turned and, for the first time since he'd been a boy, ran away.

Pete made it to the end of the next street over before he stopped, huffing and puffing.

How could I kill Belle's husband? he thought as he leaned against the wall of the last building before the end of the town. Even though he was being paid, and good, he could never hurt Belle again. Even Pete could figure out that killing the father and then the husband of the woman you loved was not the fastest way to win her heart. He didn't care what anyone said or thought. He could never hurt Belle again.

Pete spun on his heel and marched back into town, upright and sure in all the four-foot-and-change swagger he could muster.

He walked into the general store in the middle of town and cried at the top of his high-pitched voice, "Scruggs!"

"I'm right here," Scruggs replied, appearing at his side and making Pete jump. "No need ta yell. What ya want?"

"I'm here ta return your money, Scruggs. I ain't gonna kill Barnes for th' likes o' you."

A woman standing by the barrel of potatoes gasped and hurriedly ushered the little boy in front of her out the door.

"Would ya shut up?" Scruggs harshly whispered. "Let's go in back an' discuss this like reasonable gentlemen."

Scruggs gestured for Pete to lead him into the back office, but turned around and held his Colt pointed down at Pete's chest. No chance he'd miss.

"You miserable excuse for a hired gun," Scruggs snarled. "Whaddaya think you're doin', goin' back on our deal? That miserable SOB's stealin' my shipments right under my nose! He set fire to my dog's house! I'm watchin' my customers crossin' th' street to go over there cause he's cuttin' prices just to steal 'em. You can't go back on our deal! We shook hands, for gosh sakes!"

"Look, I ain't gonna duke it out with you, Scruggs," Pete explained, as he held out the bankroll the grocer had given him. "I jus' wanna git outta this town an' go back ta Polly Pocket Point with what little's left o' my dignity."

"You kill Barnes, or I'm'a gonna kill you. I'll give ya 'til tomorrow noon. Now git 'n' do the job I hired ya fer."

Pete, not knowing what else to do, turned and left the store, but not before reaching up and placing the wad of cash on the counter with deliberation.

Pete went back to the saloon, and tossed another nickel onto the counter to get himself another whiskey. If he *was* going to have to kill Barnes, he didn't want to be sober for the event. After several more, he'd found his courage, or at least a reasonably intoxicated facsimile of it. In his blur, Pete decided to go looking for the next notch on his shiny, brass plated pistol.

It didn't take him long to stagger over to Barnes' store. He stood unsteadily out in front and taunted his rival.

"Bruce Baines! I mean—Barnaby Bruce—uh, Bryce Barnes!" he yelled in false, inebriated bravado. "Come out 'n' face me like a—somethin' or other...oh yeah, a man!" Upon completion of this statement, Pete promptly fell on his face in the dust.

He rose unsteadily to his feet as Barnes walked out of his store to face the cold-blooded, soused killer before him. He was tall, Barnes was, at least seven foot of hardened muscle like a steam locomotive on steroids, rippling with looming menace. His frosty, steel blue eyes gazed across the dry, dusty road as he held up the faithful old long-barreled Colt revolver he'd had since he was a toddler.

"All right, Malaria Pete," he spat like vinegar. "Time ta see who walks away from this and who ends up in a white silk-lined, elegantly varnished mahogany box." He holstered his weapon as he finished speaking.

"Wow," Pete breathed in alcoholic stupor. "Y'all got fancy coffins like that? Must be pretty nice. How much somethin' like that run?"

"Oh, 'bout sixty dollars," Barnes, ever the salesman, replied with careless unconcern. "For five more, I can get ya the red silk lining. Very nice, especially for someone of your stature. And we can also do all the flowers as well as the hearse for just another twenty—what am I *doin'*? Get ready ta die, ya good-for-nothin' midget!"

"You're gonna be lyin' on the ground bleedin' for that insult, you skunk!" Pete roared in under-the-influence ire. "An' after tryin' to sell me a coffin, too! Get ready to eat lead, Baines!"

"It's Barnes, you dumb ass!"

"On the count of three, then," Pete fiercely challenged.

Both men moved into the ready position for the gunfight, but just as Pete reached 'two', Belle dashed out of the front of the store in tears, pleading loudly, "No! No! Don't go killin' each other! Please!"

The lofty brunette inserted herself between the two men and both lowered their guns.

"Belle," Bryce threatened, "You oughta know better'n to interfere in mens' business. Now git back inta the store!"

"I won't!" she argued then turned to Pete. "Please, dearest Pete, don't hurt my husband. I'm beggin' ya."

Resigned, Pete turned to go, placing his gun in the holster. Unfortunately, the gun went off right then, the bullet hitting him in the foot. Belle rushed to his side as Bryce erupted in gales of laughter. The gunslinger hopped around like a drunken, wounded rabbit as he yelled a stream of gibberish.

Catsup came running, thinking his master was calling him, and stomped Pete's other foot in panic. Pete let loose a high-pitched scream. Barnes fell to the ground laughing even harder as Pete continued hopping, first on one foot then the other, yelling and cursing at Catsup, who bolted off. Belle ran back and forth from Pete to her husband, fretting as Barnes writhed on the ground laughing and Pete attempted to follow his supposedly trustworthy three-legged steed. "Whoa! Whoa, Catsup! Whoa!" His five gallon hat, a mite too large, had fallen over his eyes, and as he stumbled around he came to a large puddle in the middle of the street, almost avoiding it.

Almost.

As Pete rolled over in the mud, gasping for air, blinded by both his hat and the pain in his mangled feet, Barnes' laughter suddenly stopped as he clutched at his chest.

Pete was laid up in the doc's office for a day, then the local hotel for a piece, waiting for his feet to heal, unable to show his face in public without laughter erupting through the entire crowd. As he packed his things, getting ready to leave, he heard a knock on the hotel room door. He limped over gingerly, and opened it. He looked up—and up—to see a big smile on Belle's angelic face, despite the streaks of tears. She was dressed in black from head to toe.

"Belle," Pete gasped in utter shock, "What brings you round here?"

"I'm comin' from Bryce's funeral."

"Bryce is dead? Gosh, Belle, I'm sorry. I swear it wasn't me. Never even shot him. Swear to it on the Bible."

"No, Pete, I know it wasn't you," she answered, dabbing at her eyes with a black lace handkerchief.

Pete scratched his head. "Then...what happened?"

Belle's expression changed from one of sadness to one of embarrassment, as her cheeks grew tinged with pink. "Well, Pete, he...he kinda died from laughing."

"Laughin'?"

She hesitated once more in discomfort, as she scratched one of her big boots across the floor, making a scraping sound. "Yeah, from—from you shootin' yourself in th' foot. Bryce thought it was so funny he dropped to the ground laughin'. Died an hour later. Just came from the funeral. Was a nice one, I guess. We had a nice mahogany coffin with a white silk linin' for him t'be laid out in, an'..."

Her head was bowed down as she broke down in tears, setting her chin upon her ample chest as it heaved with her sobs.

"Barnes is dead?" Pete couldn't believe this had happened. "Oh, Belle, I'm so sorry."

"He took good care o' me," Belle confessed, "But, truth be told, I never loved him, Pete. I couldn't bring myself to see ya 'fore this 'cause I was ashamed. For him and you. I didn't wanna hurt ya no more."

"Oh Belle," Pete blubbered as he hugged her waist.

"Oh Pete," Belle cried as she leaned down and hugged him back. She looked down into his eyes as he looked up into hers, and they both instantly knew it was destiny.

The long and short of it is they got hitched, with Pete taking over running Barnes' store and, in short order, putting Scruggs into bankruptcy. Had a bunch of kids too, eight in all, four boys and four girls. For some reason, seems all the boys were as short as Pete and all the girls as tall as Belle.

THE GARGOYLE CAT

Christine L. Hardy

An airplane churned the gray, humid air over the sleeping neighborhood, crickets chirped coded messages, and fireflies blinked above the grass. Not a breath of wind stirred the curtains of Gracie's room.

Zyla, the gargoyle cat, peered down from the top of the bookshelf, wings folded along her back like Japanese fans, front paws hooked over the edge of the shelf. Her fur had been etched in thin strokes by some unknown artist thousands of gargoyles ago, when the first cat was sculpted in clay and cast for a resin mold. The same artist had pressed his thumb and forefinger together to smooth the tapering triangles of her ears, flattened the bridge of her nose just so, and left the points of her claws extended so she appeared to grab the shelf with them just like a real cat. Her green glass eyes caught a faint glow from the night light.

Gracie's hair trailed in a dark seaweed tangle over the pillow as she slept. Her fingers curled against her forehead as if she were deep in thought. Zyla longed to cuddle next to her. If she were a real cat, Gracie would stroke her fur.

Something flickered near the foot of the bed, a darker line among the shadows. Zyla blinked, then leapt from bookshelf to bureau to floor, spreading her wings to break the air as she landed on silent paws.

The shadow flicked again, disappearing under the bedskirt. It was a dream snake. Zyla crept forward, ears back, tail lashing, and pounced among the toys and shoes hiding there. It slipped

25

away from her. She leapt after it. At last she trapped the snake under a thin, glossy book and bit its tail. The snake writhed, flipping the book and tossing Zyla against the leg of the bed. She cracked her resin skull on it. Miniscule fireflies blinked in her vision.

The snake darted out quick as a thought, bit the gargoyle cat's thigh, then shrank away. Zyla hissed and lashed it with her paw, tearing the skin on the tip of its tail. In that moment it dissolved into the air like smoke, leaving its skin to collapse into a roll of dust under the bed.

Zyla slumped against the bedpost, trembling and cold. The bite of a dream snake caused children nightmares and made gargoyle cats as stiff as the resin from which they are made. She felt herself hardening a little more with each breath she took. Only the child she spared could heal her.

She forced her front legs to pull and her back legs to push, crawling into the open. Next she took a ragged breath, unfolded her wings and jumped, scrabbling to get up the covers to the top of the mattress. The blanket caught on her claws and pulled her down, sliding to the side in a heap. She tumbled down on it, dizzy and aching. With an effort she unhooked her claws and tried again. This time she was able to half-fly, half-climb to the top by grabbing at the box spring for support.

She sat with her head bowed for a moment, unable to draw a deep enough breath to fill her resin lungs, then crept up to the pillow near Gracie's chin and collapsed. The child's warm, human, toothpaste-scented breath seeped into her bones and muscles and wings. She sighed and nestled against the pillow.

Zyla blinked awake some time later. Her nose was close to Gracie's cheek. She stretched her paws and wings, finding them flexible again. She wished she could stay there all night but she couldn't risk being found in the morning. She'd lose her magic and have to watch helplessly as Gracie suffered from nightmares. So she picked herself up, licked the fur back into place where the snake had bit her, and leapt from nightstand to bureau to bookshelf. She yawned once, showing rows of tiny, curved, resin teeth, and peered down at the shadows on the floor.

THE FEATHERED MESSENGER

Shelley Szajner

A Red-tailed Hawk swooped across the front lawn. It landed on the uneven sidewalk leading up to my Victorian home at the end of the wide, tree-lined street. "Oh my God," I said aloud. *Another one? I don't believe it.*

I swallowed. Something monumental was about to happen. It was the second time in two days that I had seen a hawk, and not just flying in squinty-eyed circles miles above me, but ten yards away. I knew that the hawk was a messenger bird and as a symbol it was telling me to pay attention to important messages that were coming to me. But what messages?

I had trained my intuitive mind years ago to recognize symbols and their meaning from the many hours that I had spent studying my dreams so that I could make sense of the transformation that I was going through. The changes started happening right after my painful first marriage had ended and my young son and I had moved in with my parents. Soon afterwards the dreams came, and kept on coming, like relentless waves. Powerful dreams that reflected the huge changes that I was making in my life.

Many of the dreams included animals, and on the nights that I dreamt of a hawk, a hawk would show up the following day, usually perched in the giant oak tree that shaded half of the back yard, or I would see one flying above me. And each time that it appeared, something important occurred, like the time that my son had broken his wrist from a fall. When a hawk arrived, I paid attention.

Riveted by its sudden appearance, I sat on the edge of my office chair and watched the raptor through the unadorned window that overlooked the patchy lawn, still brown in spots from the lack of summer rain. Puzzled, I noticed that the hawk had a nest in its talons. What could the nest symbolize? Baby birds, young people, or perhaps new beginnings? I didn't know.

I glanced at the long list of unopened emails on my computer screen. I wasn't in the mood for answering emails but one of them caught my eye. I opened it and read. It was from someone claiming to be my half brother, Teddy, and he was certain that that he and I were related. He also said that he had some information about my biological father, Richard Drake, if I was interested.

Chills ran down my spine.

Two years ago I had gone on a quest to find my biological father. I solicited information about him on several genealogy sites, but when I never heard anything, I gave up looking. I had forgotten all about it—until now. I realized with sudden clarity that the email containing information about my biological father was the important message that hawk wanted me to see.

Breathe, Shelley.

Hunched over my corner desk, I stared blankly at the computer screen. I had to stay calm. I had to think this through. But my heart wanted nothing to do with thinking. It raced out of control, just like my mind.

I closed my eyes. What would it be like to meet my father in the flesh? Would he want another kid in his life? If I call him, what would I say? what would he say? He might refuse to talk to me. Could I handle a rejection like that? No, I couldn't. I hesitated to do anything, even though I longed to meet him. What I wanted more than anything was to have a loving father-daughter relationship.

But I was afraid that a rejection from him would set off the sharp, steel blades of bad memories caused by the emotionally and mentally abusive relationships that I had endured with men who didn't know how to love anyone.

I opened my eyes. Looking past the front porch, its cracked, white columns in need of paint, I gazed up the street to my parents' house, the house where I grew up.

Next to their house was where Rachel used to live, a house that always had moss growing on the roof. If it wasn't for Rachel, I thought, I might not have ever discovered the secret that I had a different father — that I had been adopted by my stepdad at thirteen months of age. Would mom have ever told me if Rachel hadn't? Doubt it. Mom preferred to keep certain things hidden away in a closet, never to see the light of day. I sighed, remembering the conversation that I had with Rachel twenty-three years earlier.

*

"I know a secret about you," Rachel said. Like an expert, she snapped the bottle cap off of the Molson with the cheap metal bottle opener that dangled from her keychain, then slipped the cap into her back pocket.

"What kind of secret?" I asked, curious, but also wary. Rachael was prone to exaggerating if it suited her mood, which was unusually somber for someone who just turned seventeen. We were celebrating her birthday with some beer that we took from the rust-bucket refrigerator in her basement, a basement that always smelled of mold and lavender detergent.

We stood in her backyard, leaning against the woodpile that was behind the tiny garage with a sagging roof that leaked.

"Promise you won't get mad," Rachel said.

"I can't promise you anything if I don't know what it is." I never completely trusted Rachel. Friends don't get into fights in kindergarten but we did, and it didn't stop there. She also competed with me for the all-important attention of boys. Her hip hugger jeans and bleach blonde locks won out over my earth shoes and mousey brown hair, but I liked my eyes more than hers. How did we stay friends for so long? Somehow we did, but at a distance. Tonight, though, there was something about her steady gaze that convinced me she might just be telling me the truth this time.

"Just promise you won't tell anyone that I told you," she said, looking back towards her two-story house. The obnoxious overhead light in the kitchen glared at us through the small window, spilling light onto the dandelions that had gone to seed during the last days of August. "My mom will kill me if she finds out."

Not able to stand the suspense any longer, I blurted out, "I promise, I promise. Just tell me already."

Rachel cleared her throat. "Your dad isn't your real dad."

I blinked. "What do you mean?"

"He's really your step dad."

"How do you know that?" I took a sip of beer, then another, swallowing the tangy liquid, along with my fear.

"My mom told me."

"When?"

"A couple of years ago."

"I don't believe you."

"I swear it's true." Rachel held up her hand, showing me three fingers, the sign we gave to each other from our days in the Girl Scouts. Her eyes, now bloodshot and glazed over, never left my face. She seemed to enjoy her new role as my liberator. More likely, she enjoyed watching me squirm with silent shock.

I used to imagine what it would be like to be adopted, but I never thought that something like this could ever be true, not for me. My mind raced with the possibility that Rachel was telling me the truth. I glanced around at the neighbors' houses, then to my aunt's house across the street. Did they know too?

I placed my half empty bottle of beer on a big stump of oak lying mortally wounded next to me. An axe bit into its dense flesh that was still wet with sap and waiting to be cut into smaller pieces, then stacked like bones onto the drying woodpile. Suddenly, beer tasted bitter.

"Don't be mad, okay?" Rachel clamped her hand around my arm and squeezed it. I knew that she was more afraid of me spilling the beans to her mom, than trying to comfort me.

I wanted to crawl into my familiar, soft bed to sleep and forget about this night and everything that Rachel had said. I was too scared to feel anything but numb, and didn't know how I should feel about something like this anyway. I only knew that I didn't want to feel it in front of Rachel.

"I have to go," I said, and sprung out of the wire gate and into her packed dirt driveway. My sandaled feet crunched on last year's acorns as I hurried home, slipping through the night shadows cast by the yellow streetlights.

It was too late to ask my mom about it. She was already asleep, and so was my dad--step dad, I realized with mild shock-- but he and I were not close, and this was the last thing that I would want to speak to him about. Plus, I needed time to let it all sink in, and gather up the courage to ask mom, not so much that I was afraid of her reaction, but more afraid that she would tell me it was true. And at that moment, I didn't want to know.

*

I sat on the bottom step of the narrow winding staircase, carpeted with a cheap Persian rug that I had never really liked. It had unraveled in spots, just like my marriage. With my feet firmly planted on the floor of the recently remodeled kitchen, I dialed the number. My hands shook. After a week of mulling over the hawk sighting and email bomb from my half brother, I decided to take him up on his offer and got my father's phone number.

"Is this Mr. Drake?" I asked.

"Speaking."

"This is Shelley, your daughter." I had butterflies in my stomach—no, a stampede of buffalo.

"Hello there, Shelley," he said stiffly. "I've been expecting your call." He sounded like a blue-collar worker, his voice deep and a bit gruff, but not unpleasant.

"Teddy gave me your number and I thought that I should call you so we could get to know each other a little." I drew in a deep breath, letting the air fill my lungs before expelling it. I was speaking too fast. Could he hear the nervousness in my voice?

"I'm glad that you did. This must be a shock for you."

"It is, a little," I laughed too loud. Now I sounded like a giddy schoolgirl. It seemed to echo all over the old house built with lath and plaster walls and impossibly high ceilings.

"Something like this is very unusual." Try mind blowing, I thought. Was I really talking to him, my father?

"Your mom never contacted me after we split up," he said, almost bitterly. But not quite. "My friends said that you didn't look anything like me, but I still wondered."

Then he added, "There were a few times that I drove by your house."

He drove past my house? Goosebumps rose on my arms as I tried to imagine what it would have been like to meet him as a child. "When?"

"The late sixties, I believe," he said. "I gave up after a few tries. Didn't want your mother to see me and cause a scene."

"Did you ever see me?"

"No, I never did."

I counted the years with my fingers. I would've been around seven or eight years old back then and too young to handle something that intense. "What do you look like?" I blurted out.

"Let's see, I've got blonde hair and blue eyes, but I'm big now, about 300 pounds," he said. "I like to eat." He laughed heartily, and I liked the sound.

I stood up and walked over to the gleaming white kitchen sink. Above it, a large window fitted with a high arch overlooked the north side of our half-acre property where a few scraggly Spruce trees grew. The obscenely long driveway also looped around three properties: my house, my mother-in-law's, who lived next door, and my sister-in-law's, who lived in the next house down. Living so close to my in-laws did not exactly mean nice and cozy, but I didn't discover this until a few years into the marriage.

I stared at the sink that was filled with half empty coffee mugs, a frying pan, silverware, and dirty dishes with bits of leftover egg drying on the plates. Marriage had defined me as the resident cook, maid and sometime nurse—roles that I didn't want anymore.

"Are you married?" I asked.

"I was once. I divorced in 1976 but never remarried," he said.

"I'm on my second marriage."

"Is it a happy marriage?"

"Yes." Not lately. I was bored and unhappy but I wasn't ready to give up my fairytale illusion that I had married my Prince Charming.

"Good. Mine wasn't. I should never have married her," he said, with a sourness that could be felt over the phone. "I should have married your mother, and regret that I didn't to this day."

I never expected to hear him say that. It never even occurred to me that he would feel that way. I imagined growing up with him as my dad, teaching me to ride a bike, cheering me on at softball games, encouraging me with my goals. What would my life have been like if Mom had married Richard Drake? I would never know.

Outside, right below the window, a shadow crossed the lawn. Instinctively, I looked up. It was a low flying hawk. Another red tail, and right overhead! I gasped, unable to hide my surprise.

"What's wrong?" he said, sounding alarmed.

"Nothing." I feigned some laughter. I didn't want to discuss my strange connection with animals, at least not yet. "I thought I saw a mouse," I lied.

"It sounded like you saw a ghost."

If he only knew, I thought.

We agreed to meet at a diner on the following Saturday. It was fifteen miles from where I lived. I hung up the phone and let the tears flow. I was going meet my father after allthis time.

What could have attracted my parents to each other, I thought, as I collected myself and began to wash the dirty, rotten dishes. Richard had a dry wit and a deep voice. I bet that captured mom's romantic heart. She was young and gorgeous when she met him. The class president and Snowball Queen in her junior year at college, she was also a runner-up at a beauty contest that same year. At twenty-something, her hormones flew without a pilot's license, and that's how I was born.

*

Mom told me her incredible story about my early life on the morning after Rachel revealed her "secret." I was sixteen and a half, failing Algebra and insecure, but I had to know if everything that Rachel had told me last night was true. And if it was, why it

33

had been kept a secret from me? I sat on the edge of the brown plaid couch across from her, still hoping that she'd tell me it was all nonsense and I could go back to being unchanged.

"Where did you hear that?" She sat on the couch with the Sunday morning paper draped over her lap and a blue mug of instant coffee in her hand.

"Rachel told me last night," I mumbled. Mom peered at me through her round sepia glasses. No emotion showed on her lightly freckled face, except for her mouth. It was clamped tight, as if she knew that this day might come and she would have to be prepared to answer questions, very uncomfortable ones.

"Yes, it's true," Mom said with a straight face.

No way. She's lying, I thought. But she didn't even flinch at the bluntness of my question. I stared back at her, speechless. My life wasn't real anymore. The foundation underneath my bare feet was crumbling. I dug my toes deeper into the carpet, holding on for dear life, the only life that I knew.

"I'm sorry that you had to find out this way," Mom said.

"Were you ever going to tell me?" I blurted out. The fresh cut flowers that she always kept in a ceramic vase on the corner table, so colorful and happy, mocked me.

"Someday."

"When?"

"When I felt that you could handle it," she said in the same even tone.

How can she be so calm about this? Her dark brown hair had been cut short and I hated it. I liked it better when it grew past her shoulders. The short hair made her look mannish.

"You're a very sensitive girl," she continued. "I thought that it was best to wait until you were older."

Of course, I was sensitive. So what? God, I heard that ten times a day! I could feel her eyes probing me, probably gauging to see how hurt I was. I avoided her gaze by looking past the see-through bamboo shade that covered the window, and across the side street to the brown three-story Tudor style house. Mom's father, my Pop-Pop, grew up in that house, and my aunt and her family still lived there. "Aunt Charlotte knows, right?"

"Yes, she does," mom said. "She took care of you when you were a baby for a little while after I went back to college to finish my degree."

"Who else knows?"

She folded the thick newspaper and placed it on the giant antique oak table in front of her, carved with intricate scrolls. It was a heavy table that took four people to lift. That kind of weight could crush you, just like the truth was crushing me.

Mom sat up and placed her folded hands with their short, unpolished nails on her lap. "Everyone in the family knows, except your cousins and two brothers, of course."

"Do the neighbors know?" I couldn't wait to tell my brothers about this. Oh, my God, I thought. They're my half-brothers! I couldn't get used to the idea of them being half of anything.

"Mrs. Mitchell, across the street, and Mrs. Crane, Rachel's mom. That's all."

I was on display like some classroom guinea pig that was born into captivity, with everyone watching her day by day, holding her and feeding her until one day she croaks, never knowing that other guinea pigs had a different kind of life in the wild. They never let her in on the secret, so the guinea pig never knew, and neither did I. But everyone else did.

"I guess you want to know how it all happened," Mom said. The tightness around her jaw and mouth had softened, along with her blue-grey eyes, which usually never failed to penetrate mine. But not this time. This time they disappeared behind the clouds.

Riveted to my seat, I nodded.

"I met your father through some mutual friends," she began slowly, as if feeling her way across thin ice. "We got along very well and started dating soon after."

"Do I look like him?"

"Yes, you have his eyes."

She took a sip of her coffee, which had to be cold by now. "I did love him at the time."

I grabbed the quilted pillow on the other end of couch and hugged it, using it like a shield to protect me against some unknown enemy. "Were you going to marry him?"

"We looked at engagement rings, but nothing came of it."

"What happened?"

She cleared her throat. Now I was clearly making her uncomfortable. "He broke up with me soon after we looked at the rings. His ex-girlfriend had come back into his life. She was jealous of our relationship, and she convinced him to break it off with me and date her again. I didn't find this out until later, but by then I was pregnant."

I squeezed the pillow tighter, pressing it against my chest to keep my racing heart from jumping out. I couldn't believe that this conversation was taking place, that this story was about me. "So what did you do?"

"I didn't discover the pregnancy until I started noticing that my clothes didn't fit right. I told your grandmother and she took me to the doctor. I was five months along and it was too late to get an abortion, so I decided to give you up for adoption instead."

Abortion? My stomach tightened. I might not be here right now if she had done that. I had come that close to death already and didn't know it. I glanced out of the window again, to the fence that surrounded our yard, holding me prisoner, now. A prisoner who wanted to escape from her life.

I swallowed hard as I listened to every word. Her face was as tranquil as the lake at the end of our street, yet hid more below the surface than I ever imagined. "But you said that you were going to give me up, Mom."

"I was, that's true, but I changed my mind," she replied quickly. Her voice cracked. "You were going to be adopted by a respected doctor and his nurse wife. I had the papers ready to go but I hadn't signed them. After you were delivered, the ward nurse brought you to me and I got to hold you and feed you a bottle for a while."

Mom was silent for a long moment. It was as if she had used up all of her words for the day and there were none left. The small grandfather clock on the wall ticked rhythmically, seemingly growing louder and louder, making the silence all the more unbearable. Suddenly she wiped a stray tear with the back of her hand. "This is very hard for me to talk about," she said finally. Her voice sounded raw. "I haven't even thought about it for years."

I felt bad for her and the pain that I was causing in making her reveal a long-held secret like this, but I was determined to find out the truth about everything.

"When I came home, I cried for two days," she continued. "Then your grandmother said to me, enough, Jane, let's go get Shelley and bring her home." Tears sprung from her eyes. She reached out her arms, gesturing for a hug. I went to her.

"I'm so glad that I kept you," she choked. "I can't imagine my life without you. You're my beautiful daughter."

"I'm glad that you kept me too, Mom," I whispered, my own face wet with tears.

I listened to the clock as it chimed eleven times. Eleven hours into the day, a day where I changed forever. I hid in my little room all day, with its striped green wallpaper that had become a cage.

Afterwards, I just buried it. I never breathed a word about it to my stepfather, and he never said anything to me. Nobody in my family talked about it. It made everyone feel too uncomfortable.

*

Years later, after I had done some healing work on myself, I developed a strong urge to find my father. I wanted to know who he was so that I could discover more of who I was becoming. And I wanted a relationship with him, if he was willing to have one with me.

The recent phone call with my father was the tipping point. I wanted to know everything about him now, so that I could fill in the missing pages of my life. I was prepared to enter the unknown forest where danger always lurked behind every shadow, but which also possessed hidden treasure. I wanted that treasure.

I gripped the steering wheel of my green Toyota and drove to the diner to meet my father. As I pulled into the parking lot, I spotted his car right away, a green Jeep. Funny that we have the same color car, I thought. I parked on the opposite side, next to the diner, where there was a little bit of shade from a scrawny maple tree. I closed my eyes, said a silent prayer, then grabbed my small portfolio of artwork, along with my camera, and got out of the car.

The distinctive cry of a hawk drew my attention upwards as I hurried across the hot pavement. Riding the thermals in a circle above me was another Red-tailed. Thrilled to see its unmistakable white speckled plumage, broad wings, and red tail, I knew that this hawk sighting was another sign confirming that I was on the right path. It gave me courage to know that fate, or God, had a hand in this, and that whatever was going to happen between me and my father, Richard Drake, was meant to be.

My father got out of his Jeep when he saw me approach. A big man was right. He was tall, about six-foot-three, and graying at the temples, but his hair was still blonde, and straight. His khaki button down shirt was open and blew in the hot breeze. Underneath was a green striped T-shirt that stretched tightly over his large belly, but what I noticed was his smile. It was warm and friendly—and looked just like mine.

We entered the diner and our waitress tried to seat us at a booth but my father insisted that he wouldn't fit in one, so she put us at a table in the back. I knocked my glass of water over as soon as the waitress placed it on the table.

"Nervous, huh?" he said laughing heartily while he helped me mop up the mess that I had made.

"A little."

He removed his sunglasses. "I'll let you in on a secret: I'm nervous too."

We stared at each other across the table. I took him in, and he did the same with me. We have the same eyes, big and round and blue. And we share the same high cheekbones, but not the nose. I definitely got my nose from my mother. "I can tell that we are related," I finally said.

"Yeah, you're my kid alright." He nodded then winked at me.

I really like him, I thought. Did he like me too?

He removed his reading glasses from his shirt pocket, slipped them on, and read the menu. "Know what you want?"

I fumbled for the menu and scanned the food. I was ravenous. When the waitress came over, I ordered my standard diner fare, a turkey club with French fries and a coke with lots of ice.

"I'll have the chicken pot pie," he said to the bony waitress. He grabbed my camera from the table, and said to her, "Hey, would you mind taking a picture of me and my daughter?"

"Sure," the waitress replied.

I hesitated getting up. I hadn't even shaken his hand yet. He slid an empty chair next to him and motioned for me to sit there and as soon as I did, he put his arm around me. I leaned into my father and allowed myself to feel his strong arm protectively around me. It felt really good.

The waitress snapped the picture of us and handed the camera back to me.

"Well, here's to the first hug from your father," he said, giving me a longer squeeze than expected. He wiped the tears from his eyes with the paper napkin that was on the table.

We ate our food while we looked through the childhood photos of me that I had brought, and the family photos that he had. "Do you have any pictures of you and my mom together?" I asked.

"No, we weren't together that long." He speared his fork into his potpie and shoved a giant piece of it into his waiting mouth. A bit of crust dangled from his neatly trimmed moustache. "How is she, by the way?"

"Good," I said, wiping my mouth with the napkin.

"Does she know that you're sitting here with me now?"

"Yes. I told her that I was going to meet you."

"What did she say about that?" He looked at me expectantly.

"I don't think she's happy about it."

"I know that your grandmother wasn't happy with me a long time ago."

"What did you do?"

"It's what I didn't do that caused the problem." He leaned back in his chair. "You see, when your mother got pregnant, I didn't know about it until your grandmother came to my house."

I put down my sandwich. "She came to your house?"

"Yeah. She wanted me to marry your mother," he said. "And when I told her that I couldn't, she started begging me."

"Why didn't you marry my mom?"

"Because I made a bad choice." He reached his hand out and covered mine. "I chose the wrong woman. I'm sorry for not being there for you, Shelley. I hope that you can forgive me."

"Of course, I can forgive you." I placed my other hand on his and gently squeezed it. He looked genuinely sorry. I couldn't hold a grudge against him for this. I was grateful just to have him in my life.

I leaned forward, and half whispered, "What was my mom really like back then?"

"A wild woman," he suddenly roared with laughter, and I smiled. "She was a good woman, Shelley, and I respect her for the way that she raised you." He pointed to the portfolio I had brought. "What's that you got there?"

"My artwork. I'm an artist."

"Let me see it."

I handed him the black binder and he flipped to the first page, a highly detailed pencil rendering of a Red-tailed Hawk standing at her nest with four baby chicks. The drawing had won second place at an art show at Camden County College, where I had been a student during the early 1980s. At that moment, I realized that hawk had been with me for a long time, longer than I had realized, and he really was an old and trusted friend.

"Wow, you did that?" he said with awe.

I beamed, not only from his fatherly praise, but also from feeling like I had come full circle. Like one chapter of my life had ended and another one was about to begin. The feathered messenger had signaled a new beginning, and I gazed at the penciled drawing from so many years ago with amazement.

He leafed through the rest of the portfolio then put it down. He stared at me with soft, loving eyes, and said, "I'm proud of you, Shelley."

I blinked back the tears. I told myself that I wouldn't cry, but there was no stopping it now. I couldn't if I tried. No man had said those words to me before. It felt strange to hear them at first, but it felt good too, like a warm sunbeam that shines into a child's darkened room for the first time.

I reached over and hugged my father. "Thank you, Dad."

Barbara Godshalk

YARD SALE

Barbara Godshalk

It's finally over. All of that work and preparation for one day that flies by in a wink. There were decorations, champagne glasses, and even a pair of white shoes. Mother and daughter were working frantically to prepare for the big day.

We made our signs, put them out, and went to bed early. The yard sale was ready at last. No, this was not a wedding, although people were getting emotional. Okay, that was mostly me. "Are we done yet? Is that the last box? How much more crap do we have to put out?" "It's 7:15 AM! Didn't the sign say 8 AM? I hate early birds!" "Can you believe she wanted me to give that to her for two dollars? Is she nuts?!"

Unlike a wedding, the preparation took weeks, not months. For a yard sale, even weeks is a lot of time to prepare. Fortunately, we had a couple of cattle prods to keep us motivated.

It had been an obnoxious winter. It seems we had caught some form of a flypaper germ from hell that wouldn't die and passed it between the three of us for about seven weeks. My family doctor was wondering if there wasn't something wrong with our home.

Unfortunately, this got me thinking. (Danger, Will Robinson! Danger!) What if he's right? Why do I keep getting sick? Do we have mold in our basement? Should we move? Do hazmat suits come in toddler sizes?

We bought some HEPA air purifiers and used them religiously until we calmed down. I talked to a contractor friend, who agreed to take a look. While we did have some mold, it wasn't man-eating. He seemed to feel that it wasn't anything a good stiff bleaching and sealing couldn't fix. I happily told him to have at it and just let me know when and how much. The caveat: if we wanted the basement done, everything had to come out. "Everything?" I asked. "Yep, to the extent you two can move it," my contractor friend said.

This was the beginning of our Brussels sprouts project, painful to go through but good for you. But I began daydreaming. What if we redid our basement? It's already got a painted floor. (Danger, Will Robinson! Danger! Danger!) Martha Stewart visions were dancing in my head until reality set in. How do we really use our basement? Isn't it pretty much where we hide all the junk we throw in Rubbermaid tubs when we clean up for company? Throw in a lot of excess grocery items and my father's Lionel train collection and that's pretty much it.

OK, so much for my dreams of an entertainment cave. Looks like I'll settle for some organized storage and a play area for our toddler. So we start hauling stuff out of our basement. I am contemplating the future of each item we bring up.

I notice that my local community hall is having a yard sale on the 30th of April. They're going to have a huge draw. We could piggy back on their sale and have ours the same day. I called my mom and let her know. It was like calling a fellow crackhead saying, "I just got a great score, come on over!" There is an inexplicable mental illness involved with flea markets and yard sales. I'm convinced if there's a gene for it, it's been in my family for generations.

The current level of insanity has to do with the fact that had my mother and I gotten jobs in Honduras sewing sneakers we would have made more money per hour than all the labor we put into this sale versus the money we made—and we had a record sale. The history of this irrational behavior goes back to my childhood.

I do not have memories of being a mall rat. I was a flea market rat. More than likely this was a discovery my parents made early in their married life. They were very young and my father was not good with money. From a buyer's perspective, especially a kid, this was great. I didn't need permission to buy most things since the risk of me spending all I had was low.

When my parents had their first flea market it was the beginning of their addiction. People were coming to them and giving them cash for their stuff. Common sense cannot compete in the face of that kind of magic.

Once I was old enough to understand it myself, I was sucked into the vortex. Several years ago, when I was in a close relationship, I introduced my then-boyfriend to that world. It was a bit of a culture shock for Al. He would later joke—sort of—that he didn't know what cheap was until he met me.

Going to the flea market with us one side of his "education." He was amazed by what people were selling. When he witnessed my parents' yard sale at their bungalow in the Villas, he was amazed by what they were buying. "Shit! That guy just bought a box of shit!!" Now bear in mind that my parents were not literally selling fertilizer but small amounts of miscellaneous doodads, thingies, and widgets; some broken, some not, some with no discernible purpose to Al—or me for that matter. My dad's tool bench, and the stuff harvested from it, was a whole other realm for two clueless accountants.

He didn't have much of a sense of humor when my dad put the For Sale sign on his car. My dad and Al got along but my father was the biggest smartass on the planet and I guess he just couldn't resist.

Many yard sales have since come and gone. Some sales were nice and we made a decent amount of money; others, not so much. As we prepared for this most recent sale, we contemplated retiring from the third world wage yard sale business. We made $345.00 this time—a family record. See you next year.

*

Epilogue: It's been a year and another yard sale later. We made $40.00. Maybe I should learn to sew sneakers.

LEAVING THE LEAVES

Joanne Costantino

Every year I have the same argument with my family. Every year, as soon as the leaves begin to change color, one would think we are expecting a blizzard. The anticipation of how much of a mess the leaves will make is unbearable to them. They linger by the windows, gaze out and watch for days into weeks, seeing and monitoring how the leaves are falling and wonder—out loud—how and when the leaves will be cleaned up.

Every year I say the same thing, "Leave the leaves." Their reaction is the same every year too: "WHY?" More of a whine than an inquiry. I never understood the purpose of raking up dying leaves only to expose the drying grass. It seems to be a wasted effort.

Autumn is my favorite season. Personally, I have always liked the look of a pile of leaves. I like the crunch under my feet as I shuffle through a nice pile of tawny crisp leaves just waiting and ready to be pulverized for their end purpose of food for the earth. Then there's the smell of moldering leaves, musky and woody, to remind you that they have almost finished their life cycles and are ready for the last stage of their seasonal performance. Why not wait until the show is totally over?

The best collection of falling leaves is under our maple in the back yard. Every year it is a spectacular transition of dark green to blazing red to a brilliant yellow that almost glows in the sunlight. When the leaves begin to lazily waft to the ground they go from the yellow to a rich tawny gold where they collect in an almost perfect ring around the base of the tree, like a skirt that's just dropped from a waist.

This perfect pile calls for some action. I get out the little-used leaf blower and make a pile of all of these leaves on one side of the tree. The family is all in a giggly dither, thinking that I have finally come to my senses and cleaned up the leaves. Once the pile is in place, I gather up my camera and my granddaughter Meghan, affectionately known as "Todzilla." Once we're at the pile of leaves I say to her, "Go ahead, jump in." So she does.

"NO!" hollers her mother. "She'll get dirty."

Well, *that* was my intention, and I was going to make sure that it happened. She needed to get dirty. She needed to let loose. I don't call her Todzilla because she's a peach of a child. Her happy moments are few and far between.

As she jumps in, she giggles, and mentions how it smells good. Yep, I'm on to something, I think to my not-so-humble self. "Go ahead, dig down, throw up handfuls of leaves," I tell her. First she looks to her Mommy and then spots my camera. Oooh, a Kodak moment. Todzilla loves to have her picture taken.

As I snapped photos, she found rapture in throwing something up and down and around and not getting yelled at for it. She threw those leaves like confetti, over and over, digging down to the ground and throwing as much as her little hands could shovel up into the air, up and over her head. When she was all done I insisted we leave the pile where it was.

Over the winter they moldered, and spring cleanup revealed a giant bare spot on the lawn. I was reminded that this was *my* fault for building the pile and leaving it.

I whipped out the pictures of the captured rapture and we relived that fun autumn afternoon. The grass will grow back.

HOLE IN THE SKY

Amy Hollinger

In my parents' backyard, there's this big tree. More than 200 years old, by some counts. There are branches that have fallen down that are at least 150 years old.

It's a willow oak, my father says, and if you look at our neighborhood crookedly, you can see a line of five of them, that follow the original line of the street. Back when the area was all farms and the park at the end of the street was a forest with a lake in it. Sentinels of the neighborhood in days gone by. They are all massive trunks you can't reach around, sops so tall they block out the light. The two at the end of the row are in the park, and it's obvious they have seen many rains and storms and years pass.

The one at my parents' house is similarly maligned by time and trauma. One tree surgeon thought it was two trees grown together, and the massive trunk—nineteen feet around—splits into two large ears about twelve feet off the ground. Branches as wide across as most of the sweetgums that line the opposing fence spur out at all levels and in all directions. The top of the tree is so high and so thickly-leaved that you can't really see where it ends.

The tree was already ancient when my parents bought the house, over thirty years ago, and it took up a huge corner in their half-acre backyard. The tree was on the western side of the house, same as my bedroom. The sight of its two-eared trunk filled most of the view from one of my windows. The other window, around the corner, let in some midday sun, although one long limb blocked a bit of it. But the bulk of the tree shaded the house (and my window) from the west, and much of the

49

neighbor's house and the street just beyond. Too tall for a tree house, although my sister and I tried repeatedly, nailing wooden boards as high as my eight-year-old arms could reach. I never did get up to the crook where the trunk split, although I tried hard enough. Instead, my father built us a small play house underneath one of the largest limbs, and the tree watched over our adventures and squabbles with a gently impassive demeanor, the tall canopy swaying with the wind and providing ceaseless shelter from the sun.

One long limb, 40 feet long, used to reach out over the pool, roofing innumerable childhood adventures, but a decade ago that split in yet another storm and had to be removed. An owl used to live on that branch, near the trunk; I remember floating quietly on my back in the summer twilight, listening to him hoo-hooting softly, high overhead, as the bats zipped across the pink and purple sky.

After that limb came down, the tree was off balance. The branches were clustered on the opposite side of the tree, weighing it down, and a few years back they noticed a black slash would appear after a rain. My father investigated, and discovered a big crack between the two trunks, causing water to leak through the tree. Slugs, fungus, moss, and lichens clung to the wet streak, further decaying the poor tree so the black streak stayed black, even in the dead heat of a humid South Jersey summer.

And then just last month, the tail end of hurricane season blustered through, and one of the limbs that stretched towards the front of the house broke, landing by some miracle in a fashion that caused no damage. My mother was horrified and amazed. A twenty-five-foot section had peeled right off, leaning rather gently on the ground at an improbable angle. Ten feet closer to the trunk and the new fence would have been destroyed. Ninety degrees to the left, and our neighbor would have had a hole in his roof; ninety to the right, the sun porch underneath my old bedroom window would have been smashed.

My parents' tolerance of such near-calamities has decayed in the same way as the tree, so after a night of what I imagine were worried conversations, they decided to take the whole thing down. My mother's fears were justified when the tree surgeon discovered the heavy southern limbs riddled with carpenter ants and the crack between the two trunks nearly a foot wide and more than ten feet long.

Watching the destruction of our old childhood friend was a sad adventure. The surgeons moved up to the top first in a crane; then, using a winch & pulley, coolly and mathematically hacked away at the topmost branches; then systematically chewed off the ends of the longer, lower limbs. One fellow did most of the cutting, leaping through the treetops with a chainsaw—the antithesis of the wood fairy, in red plaid flannel and steel-toed boots. Others on the ground collected the debris, lowered to the ground by the flannel fairy with tightly knotted ropes.

The whir of the chainsaw and the wood chipper lasted three days. The first night after the tree fairies left, I contemplated the backyard. Many of the large, leafed branches were left on the ground, and a gentle wind blew through the foliage more loudly than at the top of the tree; the ragged breath of a dying tree spirit. From the ground, most of the tree still looked the same, but the gathering of twilight revealed more than I was accustomed to. From the second story bedroom where I'd spend many childhood evenings watching bats and fireflies outside the window with trunk and limbs and leaves as a backdrop, the difference was marked. The moonlight threw different patterns on the roof of the sun porch below, and even the flight of the bats was erratic.

The buzzing continued for two more days. On the last night, only the stump remained, a slab of fresh yellow wood, smelling like damp earth after a rainstorm with a twinge of gasoline from the ceaseless motors. I could lay across the stump with room at my head and my feet, although even after its destruction the tree still resisted me climbing it, the four foot platform just tall enough to be difficult. There was a stripe of softness through the center, where the crack had been, a grey streak contrasting with the pale yellow wood.

The following day, all that remained were hunks of wood, scattered in huge piles around the backyard ready to split, and a vast pool of wood chips. The ground was as flat as if the tree had never existed. But other signs of the tree's legacy remained. Four slender pines in the neighbor's backyard were revealed to be scraggly and crooked, full sunlight never having reached them. A row of hedges separating the backyard from the front were a vivid green in the sun, not the mottled dull darkness we had seen while they were in the shade of the tree. The small corner behind where the tree had rooted was dank and mossy, an area that extended into the neighbor's backyard, heedless of the man-made fence, an insignificant human-drawn line that the tree had obviously mocked. The squirrels were baffled; many of them stopped and started and turned themselves around trying to figure out how to get to the safety of the treetops without the ancient sentinel, and the birds seemed lost and chattered their annoyance.

The difference was even more defined in the moonlight. A waning moon threw full silver beams like a flashlight into the second story bedroom window, and the expanse of wood chips gleamed in the reflected light. My childhood bedroom had never seen so much moonlight.

The next morning showed more subtle changes, primarily a difference in the light patterns of the dawn rising on the opposite side of the house. As I approached the house after a morning walk with the dog, with the sun swinging towards its western bed, the house grey in the shadows of trees beyond, there was a definite difference. The entire landscape was changed, as if a crater had knocked out the treetops. The tall tips of the branches had towered over the house by a hundred feet, and its solid wall of branches provided a reassuring backdrop at least twice that distance. But now, only the neighbor's scraggly pines and the tops of trees further away were visible.

We returned to the backyard, the dog distracted by the unfamiliar smell of fresh-cut wood, and I dropped my head back, as I had done so many times as a child. The sweet smell of the wood chips filled my head and I closed my eyes. But instead of searching the branches beyond my reach for scampering squirrel or the red of a robin, there was only the sun, bearing down sideways through the hole in the sky.

PHONE CALL

Kitty Bergeron

Martha Passel sits in her rocking chair, watching her third hour of soap operas. In this episode of *La Casa*, Maria, the wife, has just found her alcoholic husband dead in her car. She opens the car door, his body falling out and slapping on the sidewalk. She falls to her knees, screaming, "No, no, no! What is it that I had done to you, Alejandro? What is *it*?"

Martha frowns and turns off the television. She looks down at her lap, smiling at the progress she has made on the navy blue blanket for her newborn grandson, Noah. Her daughter, Erin, is coming over in half an hour. Martha has been looking forward to this for weeks. She hasn't done anything besides work on Noah's blanket and watch soap operas. She has already made cookies; they are cooling on the stovetop.

Ring a-ring a-ring!

Ring a-ring a-ring!

Martha puts her knitting by her feet and picks up the telephone. "Hello?"

The other end crackles like a candy wrapper.

"Hello...is this Martha Passel?" an authoritarian voice bellows.

Martha straightens her neck, smiling. "Yes it is."

"Hello, Martha. This is Officer Black."

"Oh, hello officer! How are those brownies I made you? It was a new recipe, so I hope they were—"

"I have some bad news for you, Martha."

Martha's heart drops to the floor. "What...kind of bad?" She bites her bottom lip.

"Your daughter, Erin—we found her driver's license in her purse in the passenger seat—she got in an accident with her son, Noah, down on Hacker Avenue. A drunk driver came right behind them and the force slammed the front of the car right into a tree."

Martha runs her hand through her hair. "They're all right, right?" She holds her breath.

Office Black sighs. "I'm afraid not, Mrs. Passel. I am very sorry to tell you that Erin and Noah are dead."

Martha gasps, putting her other hand over her mouth. "Oh my lord...." She presses her hands on her cheeks, the phone between her shoulder and her ear. "Should I come over to claim her body now?"

"Well no, her husband...Nathan is here for that. He told me to tell you that he'll take care of it." Pause. "I'm sorry for your loss, Martha; I really am. I know it must be so sad to have to go through this a second time."

Her eyes begin to water. "Thank you for the information, Mrs. Black. Have a nice day." She hangs up, and puts the telephone down on the arm of her rocking chair.

She gets up and walks over to the television, where there's a shelf of older pictures, her favorites. One picture is from Erin's prom. Martha stands behind Erin, who is in a purple gown with ruffles along the side. Her prom date stands to the right of Erin. The spot where the father would stand is empty.

The picture next to that one is with Martha, Erin, and James, in their back yard on the Fourth of July. There, Erin is just a toddler with brown pigtails. James doesn't have a Bud Light in his grip; instead, he holds Martha's hand. Martha is still Teacher of the Year.

Erin is alive. James is alive. Martha is alive.

She looks back to her rocking chair, seeing Noah's blanket one last time.

It's such a beautiful blanket.

She looks away, wiping the tears with her empty hand. She looks at the photographs one last time.

Erin is happy. James is happy. Martha is happy.

She turns away, waddling into the hallway adjacent from the television. She climbs up the stairs. There are thirteen steps in all.

She reaches the top, clutching the railing. She sighs. She looks down, edging her heels almost off the ledge.

Martha lets go, and falls from the clouds of safety into the earth of risk.

Her chest smacks against the carpet; it is concrete seeping into her ribcage. Her neck snaps back. Crack.

Crack.

She closes her eyes. She has no thumping heartbeat; it is only a quiet murmur, like the whispers of wind in a graveyard. Her arms are splayed, her neck twisted to the left.

Everything fades into darkness.

Ring a-ring a-ring!

Ring a-ring a-ring!

Ring a-ring a-ring!

"Hello, this is James and Martha Passel. Please leave a message, and we'll try to get back to you as soon as possible. Thank you for calling!" Beep.

"Hi Mom, this is Erin. That was not Officer Black who called; it was a mental institution patient. They told me they knew you from when you taught at Hawkins High School. They also told me they called due to…some sort of rivalry? Apparently you rigged the ballot in order to win Teacher of the Year, but I think she was just bluffing. Anyway, I'm perfectly fine. I don't know how the patient came up with such a story. Maybe it was something with Dad—anyway, I was shopping with Noah for diapers when the patient called. Officer Black found me at my house when she was coming over to tell Nathan about the phone call, after a nurse at the mental institution caught the patient with the phone without any supervision. So now I'm at the police station to help with the investigation."

Pause.

"Well, I hope everything's okay over there; you must have been terrified. But I'll see you soon! Noah is so excited to see you and his new quilt. I love you, Mom. Bye."

NO FUN JOE

James Knipp

I didn't notice Joe sitting in the suite's small kitchenette until after I came out of the bathroom. You can't blame me for missing him. I had awakened from a dead sleep moments before, my stomach announcing the rapid, forced evacuation of last night's debauchery, and my focus was on getting to the toilet before giving Bally's another reason to keep Joe's security deposit. After what seemed like an eternity embracing my porcelain lover, I washed out my mouth and stumbled back into the main room of the suite, surprised to find Joe awake, rocking back in the scarred wooden chair, and staring intently at the bottle of Black Kraken he held in his hands.

Something about him sitting there and holding that bottle made me uneasy. Joe was married to my sister, fifteen years my senior. I'd known him nearly my entire life, and as far as I knew, he never drank.

"Hey Joe," I rasped, my voice sandpapered by whiskey and cigars. "You finally taking up the bottle?"

He glanced up and my unease deepened. His eyes were damp and far away and the grin pasted onto his face looked more fitting on a dead man.

"Did you know Black Kraken whiskey was the last drink I ever had?" His voice was as distant as his eyes. I shook my head. I wanted to make a joke, perhaps say something about such cheap rotgut being a poor choice for a last drink, but nothing came.

57

"I had a brother, too, once," he whispered, pointing the neck of the bottle at my twin, Jason, who was passed out on the floor behind me. "He would have only been a few years older than you two."

"What...what happened to him?" I asked, suddenly sure I knew and not wanting to hear it.

Joe ignored me and turned back towards the table. He spun the cap off the whiskey, reached over the small dinette, and dragged an empty Solo cup towards him. He poured, one finger, two, upending the bottle until the sixteen-ounce cup was filled nearly to the rim.

"Joe...you're not going to drink that are you?" I asked.

He fixed me with another dead look and I winced, remembering the night before. Jason had taken his best man duties seriously, trying to force shots on everyone, including Joe, whose declinations were met with good nature at first. As the night wore on, and Jason had become increasingly drunk, he seemed to take Joe's sobriety as an offense.

Joe had just smiled, and continued to do what Joe always did. He took keys. He smoothed over hotel management when the noise complaints inevitably came. He helped people find a place to lie down when they finally had enough. I don't remember all of it, but I do remember Jason's hectoring cry throughout the night.

"You're just a no fun Joe, aren't you? A real no fun Joe."

And now this man who had come into my family when we were six and struggling with the loss of our father, who had pressured the insurance company until they finally relented and paid what was owed us. The man who had convinced me to stay in college when I wanted to drop out early and work full time, and who had presented me with a substantial start up check from money he had begun putting aside the day after I told him I wanted to start my own game company. This man was sitting in a hotel kitchen looking like he was about to cap my bachelor party by drinking himself into a coma.

"Joe, man. Are you OK?"

He brought the whiskey to his lips, paused, and sniffed deeply before placing the cup back onto the tabletop.

"He could be a little shit, sometimes."

For a second I thought he was talking about Jason and I nodded, but then he added, almost to himself, "Allen. His name was Allen.

"He was a foster kid, came from an abusive family. My parents were going to adopt him."

He brought the cup back up and I tensed, but again he only inhaled deeply, seeming to breath memory from the fumes.

"I wasn't a very good son, and I positively sucked as a big brother. All he wanted to do was tag along with me, but I was seventeen. I had parties to go to, too many friends to hang with. I didn't need some little kid following me around."

He laughed hollowly.

"Except for that one time. Thought the guys would get a kick out the little shit and his smart-ass answers. I made him wait in the car while we passed the bottle around. This bottle."

He held up the Black Kraken.

"Do you know how they say, God looks after drunks and small children?" I nodded mutely.

"Well it's bullshit. He looks after the drunks, but He doesn't give a shit about small children." He shrugged.

"I don't remember getting in the car. Don't really remember anything until we were sitting in the hospital room, me with a little cut on my forehead and a broken nose, Allen swaddled in bandages hooked up to those machines..."

He looked at me with those empty eyes, and I shuddered.

"When they turned the machines off and there was this absolute silence at first. The quietest moment ever. Just a complete cessation of sound, like everyone in the world had stopped and held their breath...and then it was like in the hospital shows, you know, beeeeeeeeeeeeeeeeeeep."

He wiped his face and sighed.

"I dream about that sound all the time."

He looked back at me, and the torment in his eyes turned my heart to ash. I stood rooted, silently begging him to stop, to not tell me anymore.

"And do you know what I told my mother as she cried and screamed into my father's arms? What I told her as the police handcuffed me and dragged me out of the room? Do you know what I said?"

His voice had risen, almost to a shout. Behind me I heard Jason mutter, "Shut the fuggup, sleepin..."

"I told my mother, 'It's not like he's your real son.' How's that for a shitty thing to say?"

I didn't know what to say, so I stood there, dumb.

Joe stood abruptly and walked towards me. For a moment I thought he was going to hit me and I considered fleeing and locking myself in the bathroom until he went away, this crazed man masquerading as my mild-mannered brother-in-law.

"Sorry, Allen." He said softly.

He reached up and gave me a clumsy hug around my neck, placing his forehead on mine. When he let go and stepped back, the old Joe, the one with the quiet smile and friendly eyes, stood there.

"Well Big Bill, you made it through your bachelor party alive and relatively unsullied. Susan will be very happy. I think my work here is done."

He walked back to the table, grabbed the Solo cup full of whiskey, and dumped it into the little sink behind the breakfast nook. He searched his pockets, brought out the hotel card key and set it on the table.

"I put in for extended checkout, so you can hang out until noon. You should get breakfast, it will make you feel better."

He paused by the front door and looked back at me.

"I'm proud of you, Billy. You're a good man."

And with that, he exited the hotel room, his footfalls disappearing down the carpeted hall.

"That guy is such a doorknob," Jason said from behind me. "I don't know what Margie sees in him."

I walked away without glancing back and grabbed the bottle from the table, and upended it into the sink.

"Shut up, Jason," I said, as I watched the rest of the whiskey slowly circle the drain and disappear into the darkness underneath.

APPARITIONS OF MURDER

K.A. Magrowski

Wednesday morning, the telephone chimed its Beatles ringtone through the French country-styled bedroom, startling Dan McGuire from his sleep. It had been a good dream, reliving his honeymoon with Natalie. Money had been short then, and the small motel room they had shared at Niagara Falls was definitely no frills. But it had been the start of their life together and he wanted to remember that time, wanted to remember her, wanted the phone to stop ringing.

The dream drifted away as the phone stopped then started up again. He grabbed the cell lying on the nightstand. Martin Krakowski, the police chief and Natalie's brother, was on the other end.

"Martin, why are you calling me at this unearthly hour?"

"Noon? It's noon, Dan," Martin said.

Dan looked at the alarm clock. Sure was.

He sighed, struggling to sit up in bed. Perhaps he should give up the six-pack of cinnamon buns on Sundays. "Any reason you called or did you just want to bust my balls at the crack of dawn?"

"It's noon...but anyway, yeah, I called for a reason." He stopped. Martin liked dramatic pauses. Dan waited, trying to reach his glasses on the table. "We found Harry Lawson."

Dan's heart rate quickened as he let out a long whistle. "Where was he?"

"Well, to be accurate, we found his body. In the Pine Barrens. Been dead maybe a week? Autopsy's pending on the cause of death."

"Damn, son of a bitch escaped after all."

"I guess that depends on what you believe in."

"Mart, now don't go getting all old school Catholic on me."

"I'm just saying. I know since Nat's death things have been hard, but I guess we don't need to go into all that."

Dan fumbled with his glasses and put them on, blinking at the bright sunlight streaming through the windows. "Nope, not at all."

*

After they hung up, Dan leaned back against his pillow. *So Harry Lawson's dead.* After all these years, maybe the victims' families might have some closure. Harry hadn't been found guilty by trial but most people in the small southern New Jersey community of Ravensboro believed Dan's story about that night.

After eating, Dan booted up some old files on the computer in his office and he began reading through his notes for *Jackson's Alibi,* his fictionalized account of the Ravensboro Murder Spree.

A little while later, a noise from the kitchen distracted him. He went downstairs to investigate. *Probably Riley, in a rare moment of activity, thinking he saw a mouse,* he thought, but he welcomed the excuse to stop reading up on the gruesome murders.

The kitchen stood empty and silent, but Dan had the distinct impression that someone had been there. He couldn't say why. Something shimmered in the corner of his eye and he turned toward the movement. Nothing. He could have sworn...footsteps sounded overhead. Dan went cold. Cautiously, he walked to the living room, opened the cabinet under the stairs, and took out his shotgun. Martin had taught him how to use one years ago, when he first started dating Natalie.

Dan mounted the stairs, placing one deliberate foot in the middle of each step, praying he had been imagining things. He walked the upstairs floor, checking each room, but found no one. Finally, he went into his office. It was also empty but all his notes had been chucked into the wastebasket. The hair on his neck stood and goose bumps formed on his arms. Nothing else was disturbed.

After a few minutes, he shook it off. *You're getting old, Dan,* he thought. *You probably knocked them over yourself.* Only he knew they had been in the middle of the desk, separated into piles. So what the hell had happened? Natalie would have laughed and made him feel silly, but in her good-natured way that always got him laughing.

Later, he made a dinner of hot dogs and beans. Halfway through his meal, a rapping sounded at the back door. Martin, in uniform, peeped through the lattice panes. Dan waved him in.

"Chief. Dinner?" Despite thirty years of friendship, he still called Martin chief—respect was respect.

Hat in hand, Martin smiled. "Sure."

The two men shared a quiet dinner possible only between old friends. Once the small talk about families and mutual friends was out of the way, the two set about to eating without much interruption. Toward the end of the meal, in between mouthfuls, Dan told Martin what happened earlier, which admittedly now sounded less threatening than it had seemed earlier.

Martin just shook his head. "You're getting pretty paranoid, old man."

Dan sat back. "I could have sworn someone was in the house. You know, you develop a feeling for this sort of thing."

Martin swallowed his beans. "Still, you didn't find anyone and all that happened was some papers were brushed into the trash. The wind probably swept them into it."

Dan shook his head. "The window was closed."

"I'm still not buying it. You're the writer, it was probably just your imagination getting away from you, especially with the news about Harry Lawson." Martin lit a cigarette and took one puff. Dan knew the rest would burn to ash. Martin had "quit" years ago, but allowed himself one puff a day.

Dan got up to make coffee, avoiding the topic of Harry Lawson. Something nagged at him all night until Martin left. Watching the chief walk down the gravel to his car, Dan peered into the night as if expecting Lawson—against all laws of nature—to come jumping out of the bushes. That night, he double checked all doors and windows, shivering despite the warm September evening.

*

Early the next day Dan went into town for groceries. He made the two-mile trip on his bike, securing the reusable grocery bag with some bungee cord over the basket. By the time he got to Shane's Fresh Market, he was out of breath and resolved not to buy any cinnamon buns or whoopie pies.

He purchased the bread, milk, and eggs that he came for (along with one small box of donuts). After he left, he was passing Angie's Candle and Gift shop when he got the feeling someone was watching him. He scanned the street. A man stood at the end, hands on hips. Something vaguely familiar about the man and his oversized hat nagged at Dan.

His breath caught. It couldn't be. Dan passed a hand over his eyes and took a few steps forward. The man was gone. Dan swallowed hard and leaned back against the brick wall to steady himself. His hands shook so much he had to put his bag down while he took a few deep breaths. Finally, he crossed the street and paused outside of Second Chance books, chewing his lip before wandering in. Cathy, the owner and long-time friend, wasn't around the front of the shop. She always had a ready ear for his stories, maybe she would be interested in what happened.

Books were squashed into the wall-to-wall shelves like overstuffed pillows, and three cats lazed it up on the chairs meant for customers. Next to the register hung a corkboard pinned with fliers and business cards.

Dan caught a glimpse of a bright magenta business card which read "Help when there seems to be no hope." He moved closer. He needed help. Things were getting too weird. "Call Madame Infante for all your personal and professional consult-ations. Tarot, palmistry, fortunes told. Accept no imitators. I'm here when all avenues seem closed."

Dan snorted in disgust at himself for even reading such a thing and walked out, distracted enough to forget to call for Cathy. But a few moments later, he walked back in and unpinned the card from the board.

*

Later that day, Dan found himself staring at a neon eye in a palm. The standard icon for "fortune tellers," he assumed. The inside of the shop was hidden from view by the black and red curtains draped artfully inside the window. It seemed like every other psychic for hire store front he had passed.

He took a deep breath and opened the door. Bells tinkled, announcing his presence. The strong scent of patchouli and musk assailed him as soon as he walked through the doorway and shut the door behind him. He was blinded at first until his eyes adjusted to the candles and shaded lamps.

"Yes, may I help you? Would you like a palm reading? Tarot reading?" a woman's voice, smooth and cultured, said from the darkened room.

"No, no." He hesitated. "I'm not sure what I came here for."

"That's quite all right. Come, let's sit." A hand lightly touched his elbow and guided him to a small table, covered in red cloth. On top lay a rectangular, wooden box. The unadorned box gleamed, reflecting the candlelight from all around.

Dan sat in one of the two plush chairs. The woman with the smooth voice sat across from him. She was younger than he expected, her dark hair bobbed, with a white streak over her right eye. She wore a conservative black pantsuit and little jewelry; a flash of a pendant at the neckline and two silver rings. Definitely not what he expected. He thought all these fortune tellers wore crazy clothes and flashy costume jewelry, with overdone makeup and fake accents. The woman in front of him would have been as much at ease at a banker's convention as she was here. He relaxed a little in his chair.

She was studying him. "Not what you expected?" she said.

He jumped with a twinge of guilt. Could she read minds? "No, not really," he admitted.

She smiled. "So why have you come to me? You're not my usual client. Not what I was expecting."

"This is difficult. I'm not sure you can help me. I doubt you will even believe me."

"You don't have much faith in my profession."

65

"I don't have faith in much of anything," Dan said wryly. "I mean, I've read up on how most so-called psychics work their magic. Plus my brother-in-law is a cop. He has some experience with fraud and con artists and such."

"And yet, you still came to me," she said.

He hesitated. It was now or never. "Have you ever seen a ghost?"

"I have seen things I can't explain. Some might call them ghosts or spirits, some might just call them unexplained phenomenon, or energy surges." She paused, considering him. "But I have a feeling you're not here to ask me about a dearly departed relative as others who come here."

Before he could answer, Madame Infante reached over and grabbed his hands. He resisted for a moment, but she had a surprisingly strong grip. She held his gaze as firmly as his hands. A tingle ran up his arms and into the rest of his body. Then it seemed like she had let go and he was floating. Everything around him blurred. Unfettered, he fell. He didn't feel any fear though; somewhere, she held him, cradled him.

Dan started in his chair. She had let go of his hands and he was just sitting at the table, his arms and legs weak and jellied, as if he had just run ten miles.

"I see that you have been touched," she said. "You are not here for any run of the mill reading. Something surrounds you. A veil of death which stalks you. A dark presence. A hunter."

He swallowed hard. Could she be the real thing? "None of this proves anything or tells me anything new," he said stubbornly.

"Of course, I know who you are. You are Dan McGuire, the famous crime and thriller writer. It's normal that certain things would hang around you—your research leads you into the depths of the human mind and the darkest paths of human depravity. But I saw other things."

Dan waited. So far she hadn't convinced him of anything. Nothing she couldn't have guessed. Well, the hunter thing was pretty close. Still, he waited to see what else she would say and then he would see.

She continued, leaning over the table to fix him with a steady and serious eye. "There is a darkness coming for you."

He coughed, trying to hide a laugh. "A little dramatic, aren't we?"

Madame Infante leaned back and shrugged. "I see what I see. You came to me. I'm telling you what I feel."

"What else do you see?" He was going to make her work for his money.

She grabbed his hands again. This time there was no floating, no disembodiment, only her soft, cool fingers holding his. After a few moments, she shuddered and let go. "This hunter is something unexpected, something the world hasn't seen before."

Neither of them said anything for a while. Dan was trying to piece together everything she said. If what she saw was true, it was obvious who this hunter was. It just didn't make sense.

Madame Infante cleared her throat. "If I may, you asked about ghosts earlier?"

He nodded and told her briefly, without too much detail, about the nocturnal visit he had experience. He also left out what he had seen in town. The less he said, the better.

"Perhaps I could come to your house? I'm most interested in your story," she said when he had finished.

Dan hesitated then nodded. He wrote down his address on a business card and handed it to her. "How much for this visit?"

She smiled. "Nothing. If I'm right about you, you will pay me back in something more important that money. As I've said, you're not my normal client and I think we can benefit each other."

They agreed to meet the following evening. He walked out of the small corner shop and into the full night. He stood for some time outside, looking up. Trying to make sense of what his life had become.

*

The following night, his bell rang promptly at seven, the time they had agreed upon. Madame Infante, this time more casual in jeans and a black cardigan, smiled when he opened the door.

"Please come in, Madame Infante. Thank you for coming."

She walked in, waving one slim hand. "Oh, you must call me Maria. Maria Infante. The Madame part is more for show. For my more typical clients." She smiled knowingly as he closed the door behind her.

He laughed. "And you call me Dan. Can I get you something to drink?"

"No, but thanks. I'm really anxious to begin." She looked around. "May I walk through your house?"

"Of course," Dan said. He would follow her, but no way was he going to tell her where everything happened.

She went straight into the kitchen and stopped, took a deep breath and ran her hands over the table. Then she crossed to the window, and then the back door. After a few minutes, she left the kitchen and returned to the living room. Dan followed, intrigued. "Upstairs. There's more upstairs," she whispered, eyes large and frightened. Dan swallowed hard and nodded.

Odd, that the only time I take a woman upstairs, it's to check for ghosts. But, his wife had been dead for five years and he really couldn't see taking another wife or even a lover at this point in his life.

As soon as they got to the top of the stairs, Dan stopped but Maria headed to his office door at the end of the hall. She stood in the doorway for a minute before turning back to him.

"It was in here, wasn't it? I can feel something here, like a trail. It ends here and is strongest in this room."

She hadn't even glanced into his bedroom or the guest room. She walked into the center of the office and stood there, eyes closed, breathing deeply. Dan watched her from the doorway as she paced around the office, fingers trailing across his desk, his laptop, his notebook, the back of his chair and then across the bookshelves that lined the other three walls.

A thought struck him. "Can ghosts, if they exist, talk?" It sounded silly when he said it out loud. Maria studied him for a moment, eyes solemn and weighing.

"I've seen apparitions before, usually in historic buildings or battlefields, the normal places you would expect to find such things. But I have never spoken to one. I've been with ghost hunting groups that have used EVP equipment but haven't heard anything that convinced me that a ghost talks," she said.

"EVP?"

"Electronic Voice Phenomenon. A device to record super-natural sounds."

Dan shuffled around the doorway, skeptical. The mention of ghost hunting groups and EVP machines made him think he'd entered the realm of new age gullibility.

"To be honest," she continued, "I don't think ghosts can really communicate with us or affect physical reality. Even if we can see them, they're on a different plane than we are. I think they're really only here as either echoes or images, just barely able to breakthrough to this plane so we can see them. Maybe those we see have enough willpower or a strong enough reason to force their way into this plane. Some may be brought here by the will of someone living, like a mother who sees a lost child. But that's only my opinion."

"Then how do you explain the papers in the basket? They didn't just waft into the trash."

Maria sighed. "I can't. Unless...unless it was a ghost with such a strong emotion that it could break through. The hunter I spoke of earlier?"

Dan shook his head, trying to think straight. "So there's nothing else you can tell me?"

"No, I'm sorry, Dan. Not without some more information."

They stood there for a minute, Dan unsure what to say. Finally, Maria cleared her throat. "If possible, could I take you up on that offer of something to drink?"

He smiled. "Of course, let's go downstairs. What can I get for you—wine, coffee, a beer?"

"Coffee would be great if you don't mind."

"Not at all."

Back in the kitchen, Dan poured them each a large mug while Riley wrapped himself around Maria's legs, purring loud. Despite the warm room, chills ran through Dan's body, every sense heightened. He leaned over to the window and pushed aside the curtain to look outside, sure that someone was watching.

"What is it? Something's bothering you," Maria said.

"I had an idea. A crazy, fantastical idea but I just wondered... Would you come for a ride with me? I want to show you something." Something had been in his house; something had dumped his papers and made footsteps, something that he never saw. And this woman knew exactly where to go. Dan also knew who he saw on the street—there was no mistaking that lumbering figure and that ridiculous hat. Talk about crazy.

Maria stood up without hesitation. Dan was impressed. For all she knew, he could be some psycho luring her to a grisly death. This also worried him.

She smiled at him. "I trust you. Let's go."

*

The ride in his truck took half an hour. They didn't speak of why or where they were going. Rather, she told him about her life growing up in London, about traveling with her first husband who was in the military and about her grown son who was living in Sydney as a surgeon. He in turn told her about his wife and his writing.

"To be honest, sometimes I don't even think it's right that I take credit for the stories in the books. It's the characters that write them. At least in the better ones."

"But you've created the characters. Artistic creation is very much an organic process. You plant a seed and life flows from that."

Dan looked over at her and grinned. She got it. Very few people did.

He slammed on the brakes as he passed the turn. "Whoops, that was it," he apologized as the car skidded and swerved on the dirt road. He threw the car into reverse for about ten yards and then turned left onto a hidden road.

The road was more like a wide, sandy path. The pine forests were crisscrossed with these, leading to forgotten homesteads and the ruins of early settlements. He had to concentrate on driving on the dark road so they said nothing else. Woods lined the road and the trees leaned in, almost in an attempt to keep them out. The road narrowed slightly as it curved to the right. Dan felt again, as he had the last time he traveled this desolate path, that any moment either the mother ship was going to beam them aboard or Bigfoot would come walking out in front of them.

"Are we almost to wherever you are taking me?" Maria's voice breaking the silence made him jump. "Sorry, I didn't mean to scare you."

"You didn't scare me. Just...startled, that's all." He wished his voice was steadier. "But to answer your question, yes, assuming we aren't attacked by aliens or Sasquatch before we get there."

Maria's eyes widened for a moment, as if not sure what he meant, then she laughed and nodded. "Yeah, I see what you mean. This is the kind of road where anything could happen."

After another few minutes, the road finally ended in the front yard of a large, two-story wooden farmhouse. Even in the dim headlights of the car, it looked long abandoned. Shutters on the upper floor hung askew, grass and weeds were dismantling the stones of the walkway that lead to the front door at nature's slow but steady pace, while the windows stared nakedly without dressing out onto whatever visitors might still approach.

Dan helped Maria out of the truck, got out his flashlight, but left the headlights on. They picked their way over the cracked walk and stopped about halfway between the truck and the house, staring up. The gibbous moon added some extra, welcome light. Maria clutched at her cardigan even though there was no wind.

"Horrible place. Are we going inside?" she asked.

"I haven't been here in a long time. Let's take a walk around first to make sure no one has decided to squat here, although the chance of that is pretty small."

Around the back of the house, more devastation lay. The silver moonlight lent an eerie sheen to everything. The grass was almost knee deep and various objects were scattered about. When they got close, they discovered rusted farm implements, the rust scraping against the hand when they were touched.

Dan walked for several paces before he realized that Maria had stopped. Eyes closed, she swayed slightly where she stood.

"I can feel something. Something similar to what I felt in your house." Her voice was shaky. "This has never happened to me before. It's almost as if...."

Dan's mouth went dry. "As if what?"

But she didn't answer. Instead, her eyes popped open and she walked to the barn some fifty yards away. Dan didn't follow right away, debating if he should take her away from here or just follow her. He realized too late that despite what had happened at his house, he still hadn't believed her to be taking more than intuitive guesses. He had thought to take her here as a joke, to prove to himself that it was all bullshit. But something in her voice now frightened him. He made up his mind and followed her, struggling to turn on the flashlight as he walked, remaining silent but cursing himself.

She pushed open the barn door, the screech echoing into the night. He caught up and tried to nudge himself in front of her, but she had already walked in. He wasn't sure what he expected. The barn itself was silent. Not even the scraping of small nocturnal animals could be heard. A slightly musty smell from the hay, now long gone, wafted over them.

Maria clutched his arm. "Murder was done here. I can feel it. Murder and worse." She pulled him back out into the moonlight and headed to her right.

Oh shit, oh no, Dan thought. But yes, she stopped in front of the pigsty.

"And here. Some of them weren't dead. I can feel vibrations." She laid her hands on the decaying wooden post fence and pulled away just as quickly. "I've never been so sure of anything in my life. I've never had these kinds of visions."

Dan shuddered. "What do you see?"

Maria buried her head into his chest. "It isn't like the way we see the world. It's something in my head. Murky, impressions and apparitions. Women's voices reaching out to me."

"You see true, all right," Dan's voice shook. "Harry Lawson murdered six women at this farm and fed their bodies to the pigs. He disappeared before an arrest could be made. His wife covered for him, provided an alibi for the times that the women went missing but there were traces in his truck. Harry was long gone by the time they came with a search warrant."

"Horrible," she whispered.

Dan stumbled away, needing to get away from this place. Bile rose up, as if everything he had ever eaten threatened to spew out. "Come on, let's go."

Maria screamed and he whirled around. "What's wrong? What's happening?" he shouted, as he ran back. She had fallen to the ground, grabbing at her throat. The screams became strangled gasps for breath, and then just as suddenly as it all started, she stopped.

Dan knelt next to her, cradling her. "What happened?" He searched her for injury but saw nothing in the bright moonlight.

"I don't know. I thought someone was strangling me," she said, panting.

He helped her up. "Are you okay?"

"Yes, let's just get out of here."

Just as they made it into the truck, a sandstorm of dirt flew into the air. Dan threw the truck into reverse, hoping all the debris wouldn't clog the engine. They sped out of the farm and back down the deserted road, keeping the high beams on.

Neither of them said anything as they drove back. The mood in the car now darkened, they kept to their private thoughts.

He drove to her apartment above the shop she owned. As she got out of the truck, the guilt hit him hard. "Maria, I'm sorry about what happened. I shouldn't have brought you there."

She leaned back in and pecked him on the cheek. "I knew what I was getting into. There's no fault here. I'm a grown woman."

His face burned. She was a pretty woman and he had been alone for a long time. He would deal with that guilt later on. "Your involvement ends here. I don't want you to get hurt."

Maria rolled her eyes. "Call me if anything happens." She gave him a level look when he opened his mouth to protest. "Just call me. Don't argue."

Dan nodded reluctantly and made sure she got in safely, before driving off. Despite her reassurances, he still felt like an ass and that bothered him as much as the attacks did.

*

The next day Dan booted up his computer. Writing was his way of dealing. His wife had understood that. He guessed she thought it better than turning to alcohol or drugs or women.

He put aside his current novel and opened up a new document to work on a short story. He had been contacted not too long ago about contributing a story for a collection. At first he had dismissed it, but now it seemed the best way to get his mind moving in a new direction.

He threw on some Simon and Garfunkel and lost himself in the words for a good two hours. Presently, he became aware of a dull thumping noise coming from below. As he walked down the stairs, an icy wind swirled from the first floor. The windows in the living room were all open, curtains swishing in the night air. A chill, not from the air, went through him. He certainly hadn't opened the windows. He closed them and then continued to look for the source of the thumping sound.

There were no other windows open, but the back storm door was opening and closing in the wind. He always locked all his doors. He reached out but stopped, unable to touch the door to close it. Finally he pulled it close, and locked it.

He found nothing else out of order and walked into the dining room. He stopped at the doorway, feeling the gorge in his throat rise. Riley the cat stood there; his back arched, fur raised, mouth pulled back in a hiss.

Dan's legs wobbled and his hands shook as he made himself move. As he brushed the cat, it fell over stiff. He knelt there for some time, unable to move. Tears ran down his face, onto the carpet but he didn't wipe them away. Riley had been old, but this wasn't a natural death—it had been frightened to death by the look of it. Its eyes bulged, staring off into some other place. He hoped they would meet again.

What was going on? Could he have left the windows and back door open without realizing it? He was a creature of habit and didn't think it likely. But damnit, Riley was dead, frightened to death by something. As he cried, a presence seemed to be standing next to him. He looked around. Nothing.

A fierce pounding at the door made him jump. He ran to the front door. Maria slammed into him, wrapping her arms around him, tears streaking her face. "Thanks goodness you're okay. I've been calling you for over two hours but there's no ringing, nothing."

He pulled away from her and grabbed the phone out of his back pocket. It was fully charged, but there were no missed calls.

"Listen Dan, I think you're in danger. I've been reading my cards. Remember what I said yesterday? Something the world has not seen before? That man Harry, he can touch the world, affect things in this realm in a way that other spirits can't. He's been stalking you, gathering power. It's the only thing that makes sense."

Dan led her into the kitchen and made some hot tea, something to calm them both down. "Lawson blamed me, you know. I had seen him the night the first woman disappeared. After I left the Toe to Toe Lounge in town, I saw his truck and a woman with long blonde hair talking to someone inside. She turned to look at me when I rode my bike past them. His wife claims I was wrong, that he had been home that night with her. Afterward, Wilma Lawson would accost me in the street and yell profanities at me. She hated the whole town since no one believed her." Dan shook his head as he strained each tea bag, then handed Maria a mug.

Maria opened her mouth to say something, but suddenly all the lights blinked and the room shook like they were in an earthquake. Dan's mug smashed onto the floor and he heard thuds as other things fell. The shaking stopped after a few moments. Neither of them said anything as they waited, knowing more had to be coming. Slowly, they walked into the living room.

Within moments, a high-pitched whine filled the room making them cover their ears. Dan was sure that if it kept up, their eardrums would burst. It stopped as suddenly as it began, and then the lights went out. Maria let out a scream—and then she was no longer at his side, holding onto his arm. Her screams faded away. He reached out, waving his arms around him, calling for her, but no answer.

His last hoarse call of "Maria!" echoed in the dark as he stumbled into a wall.

He whimpered for a few seconds, holding his right arm. For a brief horrific second, he thought he might actually cry. But then he pulled himself together as much as he could, and felt his way to the light switch. He flipped it a few times but nothing happened. He reached down to the half-moon table where he kept his keys, and pulled a small emergency flashlight from the drawer. Luckily, the batteries still worked. A quick search of the room showed Maria was nowhere to be found but the front door was still shut. *So where the hell was she?*

Dan trudged up the stairs. If it was Harry's ghost, he knew where he would find him. At the top of the stairs, he shone his light down to the end of the hallway. There was nothing out of the ordinary, although to Dan's heightened perception the hallway seemed unusually long. He felt like a condemned man walking to the noose.

At first step he knew something was wrong. It was as if he had stepped into invisible quicksand. The air grew hot and thick, hard to breathe and hard to move through. He tried pulling back but found that even more impossible so he resolved to move forward. It was difficult and at times he thought he would suffocate to death. Finally he reached the door to his office and pushed it open.

Cold ran over him like icy, dead fingers playing over his skin. His breath misted in front of him when he exhaled. His light shined on what was left of his computer. Keyboard keys and monitor shards lie scattered as well as other, more mysterious innards of the computer.

He took a small step into the room. Then a few more. Finally, he stood in the middle of the room. The rotten smell of the grave, of putrefied flesh, of open wounds, assailed him.

He slid the flashlight beam around the room and yelled, bile rising in this throat. Maria was splayed out on the far wall, iron spikes driven through her hands, feet, and eyes. Streams of blood ran down her and onto the floor. He wanted to rush over to her but instinct held him back. Evil was there, and the closer he got the worse it would be for both of them.

"Damn you Harry! Damn you to all hells!" he yelled.

The hair on his neck stood up and he whirled around. Nothing there.

"Harry! Come on! Come get me! Let's have it out you sonovabitch!"

The air thickened around him again. The room darkened, as if a dark presence was forcing all the light out. Spots danced before his eyes as he gasped for breath. Time slowed down and flashes of the past, caused by the lack of oxygen, cascaded in front of him. He was going to die, but he didn't care. Whether in this world or the next, he was ridding it of a parasite. He had had a good life and he couldn't find it in him to have regrets. Except one—involving Maria in this. And Lawson just took her away from him.

Sweet air filled his lungs again; big cold gasping breaths of air. The room was still semi-dark and he was not alone. Harry clung to him like fine-netted blackness. Whispers of air tousled his hair and passed by his ears as whatever Harry was, that blackness, swirled around him. Dan knew of no way to combat what he could only see as smoke.

The murky blackness coalesced in front him, vaguely man-shape. It waved, grew to twice Dan's height, looming over him before shrinking down to normal height. Now a cloaked man; the Grim Reaper, scythe raised high. Dan threw his arms up in self-defense as it came down at him and passed through him. A thousand daggers flew at him from every side and vanished in puffs of smoke.

Sweat beaded his forehead, his hands shook, his heart beat too fast, too hard. His right eye twitched several times as he turned in circles, waiting for the next attack. Harry was playing with him. It had to end here, had to end tonight. But he was out of ideas. Not that he had had any to begin with, he thought wryly. *Well, either way, if it ends, it ends without me acting like a rabbit at the end of a rabbit run.*

Dan walked down the hallway to the bedroom. It was all he had left. Calmly, he opened his wife's jewelry box that he kept on his bureau, looking for the one thing that might work.

His senses prickled. The darkness crept up the hall. He clutched the crucifix to his chest. He had given up her faith when Natalie died, but it was all he had left.

"Natalie," he prayed, "I know I'm not a religious man. But if you can intervene, somehow, please help me. More than just my life, which means nothing, is at stake here. You know the evil that he was and still is. Please Nat. I can't let that be unleashed into the world."

The dark whispering was coming close, he could feel the rustling, could see the darkness squeezing out the light behind him. He turned just as it came upon him and thrust the crucifix out in front of him.

"Harry! Come on! Let's see you go to hell, even if I have to take you there myself!"

The air rumbled around him, almost as if the darkness itself laughed. The smoke tried to wrap itself around him but seemed to only be able to tangle itself around his arms. Its frustration vibrated throughout the air.

Sweat once again beaded his forehead but not from fear but from heat. The air was growing increasingly hotter, and rivulets began to run down his chest and over his outstretched arms where the muscles pulsed in their rigidity. Dan gasped for air but continued to hold onto the crucifix until it became too hot. But before he could let go, the metal flared to red hot heat and Dan screamed, trying to open his hand. Finally he pulled his fingers open. The cross stuck to his palm. The air cooled and the darkness dispersed to the corners of the room. Dan sank to knees, tears mixing with the sweat on his face. He looked at his hand, palm facing up, cross burning into the flesh. He grabbed the base of the crucifix with his other hand and without thinking further, pried it off with one quick motion. His scream echoed through the house. Pieces of flesh still clung to the burnt metal.

The angry red burn throbbed on his palm. He sniffled but didn't bother to wipe his nose or eyes. Rocking back and forth on his haunches, he could do nothing but hold his injured hand and wonder when the next blow would come.

Then he heard it. At first he thought it was the darkness coming back for him. But when he looked up, he could still see it wavering and swirling in the corners of the room, as if waiting, unsure. Whatever it had expected, it hadn't been what happened. Dan wasn't sure how he knew that, but he just knew. Although his hand hurt like hell, the pain was lessening dramatically. Whatever harm Harry had been trying to do, he had been stopped.

But there it was again. A rustling noise like trees in the wind, only he could see out the window that the branches weren't swaying, and the few clouds lit by the bright moon were stationary. The noise picked up in intensity, coming closer.

"What other hell-wight have you called up," he said, voice rasping as he tried to draw more air.

Of course, the thing that was Harry did not answer, not that he expected it to, but Dan had to say something. He wanted to appear to be defiant, although he felt more like pissing his pants waiting for whatever was coming.

A chill wind wrapped around him as he crouched, a cold white fog, that cradled him and then spread itself out into the four corners of the room. The blackness that was there melded into the white and for a moment, Dan heard voices—a deep-throated scream slowly being consumed by whispers that tinkled like silver iced bells, rimed with cold comfort. He realized the dead were taking back their own.

As the crystallized wind continued to swirl around him, he reached out to either side to embrace what had saved him. The pain in his hand was gone, but his skin was raised slightly with pink scarring.

If he had hoped for some communication or answers, then he was out of luck. The wind that encircled hadn't come to save him but to devour what had been Harry. He could feel tiny ice pricks as it moved over his face, hands and arms. It seemed to want to get at whatever part of himself he didn't like to admit he had, that they all had—the darkness within himself. Something wanted to tear free from inside him. His body tensed, quivered as the cold intensified and the wind circled faster around him. Something was being torn. The air was so cold he tried to draw a breath and gasped, unable to fill his lungs. Every muscle tendon and fiber vibrated to the tinkling ice sound that filled the air again.

Then it was gone.

The air warmed and he gulped a large breath of it. His body relaxed. Unfortunately, it relaxed so much he felt his cheek make contact with the floor before he even knew he was falling forward, and blackness consumed him.

*

"Dan! Dan! Can you hear me?" The voice came from far off. Someone stroking his cheek. He pried his eyes open. Maria. She was looking down at him, eyes wide, searching his face.

"You're dead," he croaked. "Am I dead?"

Maria smiled and shook her head. "Not yet. I was dragged away and thrown into a closet by that...thing. I must have fainted."

Dan, still on the floor of the bedroom, pushed himself up to sit. Or tried to. His hand burned. He looked at his palm; the crucifix had burned itself into his flesh and his head throbbed worse than with any hangover. "But I saw you, dead."

"Illusion probably. I don't think Lawson could kill anyone— yet—in the state he was in. I think he was saving what strength he had for you." She looked around the room. "But whatever he was, it's gone for now."

Dan grabbed her hand with his good one and squeezed it. "Oh, I think it's gone for good." Justice had been served.

THE NIGHT OF THE ATTACK

Marie Gilbert

Mandy was in a lot of pain. Her right arm was throbbing and she felt feverish. The bright light shining down from the attic skylight burned into her brain, making her roll on to her side to protect her eyes. She was trying to remember how or why she was up in the dusty attic in the first place, but her mind kept drifting off.

"Mandy wake up, I'm afraid," her little brother whined as he shook her arm.

She had forgotten that Matt was here with her. She tried to speak to him, but her tongue stuck to the roof of her mouth.

"I think they're still in the house," he whispered and glanced over his shoulder at the attic door.

"What?" The fact that the intruders were still in the house helped her to overlook the pain in her wrist and head. She forced herself to sit up. Her vision was blurred, but not enough to prevent her from seeing the fright on her ten year old brother's face.

*

The nightmare had begun over a month ago. The reports from China telling of a virus that seemed to imitate mad cow disease, with people losing all inhibitions, were only the tip of the iceberg. Not until the disease reached the States did people understand how widespread and unstoppable this problem was.

*

"I don't feel so hot," she said to Matt. She would've called him a snot nose, but she was in too much pain to joke.

"Is the lock still holding the door closed?" she asked Matt. His only reply was a quick nod of his head.

*

The news reports on TV warned the people to stay in their homes, to block all their doors and windows and to arm themselves. The disease was thought to be airborne, but nobody knew for sure. What was known for certain was that those people who were bitten by one of the infected became ravenous for human flesh.

Thank goodness her father was a police officer. He made sure that Mandy and Matt knew how to safely use the hand gun. He had boarded up the windows and doors of their small home, but he knew it wasn't enough, so he added a thick drop door to the entrance of the attic. If the intruders were able to get past the barricades, then that door and its thick bolts would keep them safe until help arrived.

"If anything happens to us, you're to protect your brother," her father had instructed.

"But he's a brat and doesn't listen to anything I tell him," she's countered.

"You're sixteen and you need to look out for him."

*

She remembered her father's words so clearly now, even if the events in between were hazy. "Your arm looks really gross, Mandy," her brother said.

She glanced down at her throbbing wrist. The skin around the wound had turned a mottled grayish yellow, and the nasty color seemed to be spreading up to her forearm. She wanted to cry, wanted the nightmare to end, but her eyes were too dry.

*

They had heard the shots coming from the home two doors down, followed by the ungodly screams. There was no other warning before the crazed mob was at their door. Mandy could still hear the unnatural moaning rising from the undead as they pounded on the door of their two-story home. They thought the barricade would hold, but when the mob began to disassemble the boarded up windows, her mother dragged Matt upstairs to the master bedroom and the safety of the attic. Mandy stayed with her father, unable to leave him alone, too afraid to move.

"Mandy, go with your mother," her father ordered as he stood at the door with his gun ready. But Mandy stayed, frozen in fear, as the first wave of zombies tore down the wooden barricade from the large picture window in the living room. Her softball coach had been the first to break through. Coach Johnson was a great guy, but this wasn't him anymore. He and two other neighbors pulled her father to the ground and all Mandy could do was scream.

"Get up Dad!" Mandy cried out when suddenly her mother appeared and grabbed her arm.

"Hurry Mandy," her mother urged as they stumbled up to the master bedroom, but the zombies were fast and rushed after them.

"Take the gun," her mother shouted out when the animated dead began to break through the locked bedroom door. "Run Mandy, run!" her mother had screamed before vanishing inside the mass of ripping teeth. In the end, it was her brother's screams that finally broke through her shock and made her run towards the attic steps.

She was almost to the top of the ladder when one of the zombies who had left the feeding frenzy in the other room appeared at the bottom of the ladder. Mandy vaguely recognized her French teacher, but this was no longer the exquisite Miss Adelphi who all the boys drooled over at school. This creature, with its bloody and decaying flesh, was no longer pretty. Miss, Adelphi bit Mandy's wrist and tried to pull the girl off the ladder.

"Help me, Matt," Mandy screamed out in pain and terror. She probably would have been pulled down to her death, if Matt hadn't dropped a heavy vase onto the zombie's head. It didn't kill the woman, but it gave Mandy a chance to climb the rest of the way into the attic and drop down the door with its heavy bolt. They heard noises at the door, but after a time they subsided as the zombies lost their scent. They were safe.

*

"I'm thirsty," Matt said to his big sister, bringing her back to the present. He sat next to her and laid his head on her shoulder.

"How long have we been up here?" she asked. She was hungry and couldn't remember when she had last eaten.

"Two days, I think."

It was hot in the attic, and Matt's hair smelled of sweat, but it was the smell of his skin which interested her. She was hungry and his smell made her more so. Her head and arm stung, as if a whole colony of bees were attacking her. But the fire burning in her stomach was worse. She needed fresh air.

"I'm going to open the skylight and when I do, climb onto the roof and see what's going on," she instructed her little brother, hoping to get his tempting smell away from her.

After she had opened the window and helped him climb through and onto the roof, he called down to her. "The street is packed with them. We won't be able to run away." He began to cry.

His crying irritated her. She was hungry, and the realization that her food was a hand's reach away made her angry. "Shut up," she hissed.

His eyes went wide as he recognized what was happening to her. "Give me the gun, Mandy."

"Shut up," she hissed once more. The burning in her stomach was overwhelming and there was only one thing that would cure it. She needed to feed.

"Give it to me..." he started to say, but something in the distance had distracted him. "It's a helicopter," he yelled. He stood up and began to wave his arms over his head.

She reached up through the window and grabbed hold of his ankle. The smell of his human flesh fueled the flames in her stomach.

"No, Mandy, don't. Help is here," he said to her and then went back to waving at the army chopper.

A low growl began deep in her throat, the hunger blocking all else from her mind. She pulled his ankle and then his leg back into the attic and opened her mouth.

"Give me the gun!" She heard Matt's panic through the haze of her hunger. "Remember what dad told you. You have to keep me safe." A small part of the obedient daughter still remained and she stopped, her teeth inches from his flesh.

She pulled the gun from her waistband. Her hand was shaking as she handed it to him. "You have to do it, Matt. Do it now," she ordered as the last bit of her humanity disappeared. Her hunger took over and she opened her mouth over his calf.

She felt the recoil as the bullet hit her forehead, but the hunger was stronger than death itself and she spread her mouth wider. The second shot sent her flying to the floor and as her eyes began to close, she saw the helicopter hovering over her brother. The army sniper's second bullet did the job. and as life seeped from the back of her shattered skull, she smiled, knowing her bratty brother was safe at last.

THE JUNKYARD

William Harden

Before he tried the knob on the door marked "Office," Michael tried unsuccessfully to look through the glass panel in the door. The glass was reinforced with wire mesh and was so filthy that it almost looked like there was a shade drawn. Half expecting, and half hoping, that he would find the door locked, he was surprised when the grimy knob turned easily in his hand and the door creaked open, protesting his intrusion with an eerie sound, high-pitched and raspy, like a voice warning the visitor that he was not welcome.

The sign at the road had said "Ralph's Used Auto Supplies," a polite euphemism for "junk yard," Michael supposed. In his thirty-nine years he had never had occasion to visit a junkyard, mainly because he knew next to nothing about cars, except for the location of the little gizmo that opens the gas tank. He was certain that purveyors of all things automotive were aware of his lack of knowledge—and his lack of interest, for that matter—and most of them took great pleasure in either mocking his ignorance or taking advantage of it. He told himself that he'd gotten used to it, though, and was comfortable thinking he didn't give a damn whether they respected him or not, despite his wife Elizabeth's gentle teasing from time to time. But the discomfort remained whenever he found himself face-to-face with a genuine "car guy." And this place was a place for "car guys," if ever there was one.

As he crossed the threshold, he realized that the building wasn't really a building at all. The entire back of the "office" was open, with two garage doors raised to allow you to walk right out into the yard. In the middle of the room was a grimy counter, the front covered with worn decals from a variety of auto parts manufacturers, advertising spark plugs, shock absorbers and God knows what else. The walls behind the counter were likewise covered with half-torn posters, an ancient clock whose second hand was traveling around the dial in jerky increments, and a bulletin board with so many bits of paper stuck to it that he wondered how the pushpins kept up with them. Right in the middle of the wall, seemingly immune to the dust and grease that dominated the room, was a calendar with a picture of a woman, a redhead, nude except for a red kerchief around her neck. One foot up on a stool, her back arched, she was holding a wrench in her hand. Her haughty gaze followed him as he approached the counter and he felt a brief stab of guilt and embarrassment, certain that Elizabeth would quietly disapprove of his attention to the pinup.

Michael was startled out of his staring at Miss September when he realized that the man behind the counter was looking at him. He had an enormous belly hanging over dirty blue jeans held up by even dirtier suspenders. His once-white T-shirt strained to enclose him. The baseball cap he wore was so grimy that you couldn't read the logo on it, his gray hair escaping from the sides and the back. His face was round and unshaven; his nose red and veiny; the shape of his mouth indicative of some missing teeth. Michael could not imagine that face smiling so he doubted whether he would ever get confirmation on the tooth situation.

His gait was labored but oddly graceful. Startled by his sudden presence, Michael actually drew back a step, briefly considering a quick exit to the parking lot. The fat man looked both menacing and welcoming, a further contradiction that left Michael on the brink of uncomfortable. Michael knew the fat man was Ralph and, stranger still, he sensed that the fat man knew him as well.

Still not a word had been spoken. Ralph reached for a binder lying open on the counter, and then spun it around toward Michael, like a hotel desk clerk completing a registration.

"Name and date of birth," Ralph told him, in a surprisingly soft and almost feminine voice.

Michael signed his name and wrote his date of birth in the binder, his entry about halfway down on the page. There were hundreds of pages beneath the one he signed, the edges wrinkled and torn. He wanted to read some of the names scrawled above his, but Ralph spun the book back around as soon as he was finished, slamming it closed, raising swirls of dust that caught the sunlight coming in through the open garage doors. Michael looked down and fought back a cough.

"What can I do for you today, Michael?"

Michael hesitated, sure that his ignorance of things automotive was about to become an enormous source of embarrassment. He looked into the grizzled face of the man behind the counter, and saw nothing but understanding and patience. His unease disappeared, and Michael paused before answering.

"I'm looking for a Toyota Camry, about ten years old."

"What color?"

"Gold, sort of."

Ralph looked down at the registration book, ran his hand over the cover of the book like a caress, then looked back at Michael. "Toyotas are on the left side, about halfway down the row. Good luck, Michael." With that, the man turned and walked away.

As he stepped through the wide bay door into the yard, Michael could see for the first time how enormous the place was. He squinted through the bright sunlight but the far end of the property seemed to dissolve in the haze and he could see no end to it.

The cars were arranged in two long rows, with an aisle of sorts between them about thirty feet wide. The aisle was just a dirt path, really, with ruts and loose stones and, with each step he took a tiny cloud of dust arose. Looking down, Michael grinned ruefully; his wing-tips would definitely need a shine after this little adventure. He couldn't remember why he had chosen to wear the fancy dress shoes on this trip. Elizabeth would probably scold him, in her gentle way.

The cars were arranged neatly, or as neatly as junked cars can be arranged. The tires had been removed and the wheels rested on rims that had been turned on their sides. The cars looked like metal creatures, squatting in the dust ready to pounce when the right opportunity presented itself. The damaged grills, when present at all, added to the feel of menace, like gaping jaws, sometimes toothless, but dangerous anyway. Michael tried his best to remember what Ralph had said to him about where the Toyotas were located. He didn't want to spend any more time wandering among these rusty, threatening relics than he had to.

Michael could see that most of the cars had been marked with spray paint, either on the windshield, if there was one, or on the fender, with the make, model and year. Most of the cars were so disfigured that they were almost unidentifiable. Some looked like they had been out here for years, some as if they had just been brought in, all jumbled together in a haphazardly tidy way.

Michael soon realized that there were other people in the yard. He heard an occasional clank of metal on metal, then a dull thud like someone wielding a rubber mallet and a soft undercurrent of what he presumed to be voices, like a low muttering. The place was so huge, though, that he could not begin to tell where it was coming from, wondering if his ears were playing tricks on him. One moment there was complete silence, then a clank to his left, a thud to his right, then the ebb and flow of that unintelligible mumbling. Michael shook off a sense of disorientation and moved off down the aisle.

He saw the dust being kicked up first, then just a glimpse of another person moving from one row into the next. Michael could just make out a tall black man, well-dressed and walking ramrod straight. Then he was gone, only the cloud of dust remaining.

As he continued down the aisle, it became increasingly clear to him that most of these cars had not found themselves here because they had been worn out by their owners. These cars had been in collisions, some of them clearly catastrophic encounters with trees, telephone poles or other cars.

Doors were collapsed like accordions, roofs caved in like the cars had flipped over, leaving the dome lights in the approximate place where the driver's head would have been. Each car seemed to have its own story and Michael felt that, by simply standing next to it, he could envision what had happened to each one, almost like he was witnessing the event that had brought a once solid and reliable—or perhaps fast and sexy—machine to this place.

Shattered glass was the one constant. It crunched under his shoes, littered the front and back seats of most of the cars. Remaining pieces hung like ragged shrouds from the window openings. As he stared at a ruptured windshield, picturing the meeting of the passenger's head with the glass, he was suddenly aware of someone else's presence. There he saw another figure a few rows away from him, just a kid, maybe ten years old, hands in the pockets of his jeans, scuffing his sneakers to stir up enough dust that he seemed to be moving in a small cloud. "Your mom's going to be thrilled with your old man for bringing you to a place like this," Michael muttered under his breath. Too far away to have heard Michael's comment, the boy's head shot up like a dog that has heard his master's footsteps at the back door, and he darted into the nearest row, gone from Michael's view.

Michael and Elizabeth did not have children. They had met relatively late in life, and, by the time they married, had both had a number of years to get comfortable with the prospect of a life to be lived alone. When they met, fell in love and married, they talked of children, but, after a few years without results, they simply stopped discussing it, an unspoken agreement that they were so blessed to have found each other, they had no right to wish for anything further. Michael confessed inwardly to an occasional twinge of regret when he saw a man his age at the mall or in town with a son or daughter, but he had learned to quickly suppress it, like pinching out a tiny ember that shoots from the fireplace and lands on the carpet.

Sometimes he wondered if she, too, felt that same twinge but he never asked about it, for fear that she would interpret the question as disappointment on his part. Her happiness was all important to him, more important than his own happiness. He cherished every moment they were together...maybe a child would have deepened their love, but it was difficult for him to even imagine a greater happiness than they already knew.

Moving to the next row, Michael finally saw a car with "Toyota" spray painted on the front. It looked nothing like any Toyota he had ever seen, but it was a sign that he was getting close. He stepped gingerly down the row, looking left and right for something familiar. The rear hatchback on the car to his left was open and he leaned closer for a look inside. Feeling a bit like an intruder, he glanced over his shoulder to see if anyone was watching, but there was no one, at least no one he could see. He leaned in and froze. There before him were a couple of textbooks, some clothing, a pair of sunglasses with one lens missing, the other cracked. For a brief moment he was paralyzed by what he saw, as if the occupants of the car on that fateful day were standing there with him, broken and bleeding from the accident. He pulled back as quickly as he could, and the image was gone, but the books and clothing sat there, innocent items that one sees every day. Yet, in this morbid junkyard they were vivid reminders of the mortality of the people who once owned them. Realizing that his hands were shaking a bit, Michael stepped away from the hatchback and took a couple of deep breaths.

He moved further down the row and there, right before him, was a car almost identical to the one he had owned when he and Elizabeth first met. Same color, beige, with a red pinstripe. He'd loved that car and gave it up only when the repair costs got out of control; that and the shame of having the only car in the parking lot at work that was held together by duct tape. Elizabeth never pressured him to get rid of it, though, only dropped a subtle hint now and then. Seeing the car was almost like seeing an old friend, though he knew they had probably made thousands of them identical to the one he drove. He walked right over to it and leaned in the driver's side window. The seat was stained with what he presumed was blood and, once again, he was nearly overwhelmed by a sense of someone's presence there in the car. He closed his eyes to let the sensation pass, and he could see flashing ambulance lights and hear garbled snippets of police radio transmissions. When he tried to pull back, he banged his head and saw stars briefly before he could shake them off.

Michael was suddenly weary, as if he had been up and down every row on both sides of the huge aisle. His feet, achy inside the now filthy wingtips, were begging him to sit for a while, but there were no benches to be seen. Sitting in a car was not an option after these powerful experiences. Michael moved on down the next row.

There was a mini-van, the soccer team decal still proclaiming the superiority of the Aztecs. Next to it was a mid-size car, its make and model, even its color, made indistinguishable by the fire. Beside that was a smaller car, all four doors missing, but there, firmly fixed to the back seat, was a child's seat. Michael paused to consider that one, and, without really knowing what the Jaws of Life looked like, he could see the rescue personnel working to free the people inside. He was beginning to recognize that some of the vehicles had an aura of death and loss, while others conveyed a sense of victory, of death cheated. He was certain that the cascade of images and attendant emotions were why he was so exhausted. It was like he was being forced to relive each collision and its consequences, like a television series that thrusts the viewer into a new catastrophe each episode.

Michael found himself beside a dark blue Mercedes, seemingly undamaged until he walked around to the rear of the car and saw that it had been crushed almost flat. Elizabeth always joked about owning a midnight-blue Mercedes one day. "Fat chance," he had always told her, "not unless one of us hits the lottery." "Well," she would always reply, "someone has to win it. Why not us?" They must have had that silly conversation a thousand times. It always ended in a laugh, but inside Michael ached at his inability to buy her that car, no matter what the cost. It wasn't the status that came with a luxury car, and it wasn't some desire for comfort and performance, as the car commercials told them. She just genuinely seemed to want one. She could have joked about getting a rocket ship and he still would have felt badly about not getting her one. "I'll bet we could get this one for a good price," he said quietly as he walked off, shaking his head.

He walked, stopping to listen to the undercurrent of distant clanks and thuds. The ever-present hum of far away voices reminded him of the last few words in the theater when the lights have gone down and the curtain has gone up, indistinguishable yet impossible to ignore. Michael shrugged them off. His annoyance with the lack of any apparent staff to help him was gaining. Michael was not what you would call an impatient man, would never be characterized by his friends and co-workers as someone with a temper, but he could feel himself losing his grip, waves of anger, frustration, and impotence washing over him like he could never recall.

Michael continued down the endless rows, sometimes losing his way, sometimes drawn to a particular vehicle, then appalled by the violence, the gore, the tragedy of yet another car crash. A head-on collision on the interstate, a driver asleep at the wheel on a country road, an inattentive soccer mom with a cell-phone to her ear, the rest of the mini-van mercifully empty of passengers. They went on and on, each one more grisly than the one before. And he seemed to be a *part* of them all, not just an observer. He was *there,* somehow, connected to the cast of characters by his presence in the junkyard, by his proximity to the car.

Between each of these episodes, he wandered the junkyard, his reason for being there—his *mission*—becoming less and less clear to him, yet more and more urgent. Despite his lack of success so far at finding the car that he sought, he knew he was getting closer to what he was looking for, like he was being drawn deeper and deeper into the junkyard by some powerful force of nature. As if in agreement, the weather changed, with the arrival of thick, dark clouds moving in a stationary, swirling motion that was almost hypnotic. There was a foreboding about the junkyard now that had not been there before, and he was not sure if it was because of the impending rain or something else. Michael tried to shake off the ominous feeling.

Then it hit him, like one of the many collisions he had been forced to witness during the previous hours. There, before him, was the Toyota he had been looking for. He knew it before he even got close enough to touch it; the car silently beckoned him.

From his vantage point, it didn't look too bad actually, better than many of its neighbors, he thought. Michael took some comfort in that, and he relaxed a bit. He moved gingerly around to the driver's side and froze. The driver's door, what was left of it, was crushed, the inside panel almost touching the center console. Both airbags had deployed, but he knew that it had done the driver no good. He leaned inside and was immediately transported to a crash scene.

He could smell the spilled fuel and could hear the constant chatter of the police radios. The flashing lights from an ambulance dizzied him and the glow of the flares in the street cast a reddish glow over everyone and everything. And there, sitting on the curb, a blanket around her shoulders, holding an ice bag to her forehead, was Elizabeth. The paramedics stood nearby, but seemed unwilling to get too close, like they were ill-equipped to deal with her pain despite all of their equipment and training. She was staring at something on the grass to her right and Michael followed her gaze. There on the lawn, debris from the unsuccessful efforts at resuscitation lying around him, was the driver. Somehow, Michael found himself standing over the man. He bent over slightly, and the sight of the man's face hit him like a body blow that knocked the wind out of him—the face was his own, bruised and bloodied but unmistakably his. He looked back at Elizabeth, but the paramedics were helping her into the ambulance. After the slamming of doors, it pulled away, silent at first, then its siren screaming as if to proclaim the feelings of the woman inside.

He looked back at the broken remains of himself. Other rescue personnel had lifted his body onto a gurney and were wheeling it toward a second ambulance. The doors slammed shut and it, too, pulled away. No siren this time, Michael observed.

He drew back from the car and was once again in the dusty junkyard, but something had changed. Despite the filth and the debris, there was clarity around him that had not been present before. The suddenness of the crash came back to him; they had been laughing about something, singing along with something on the radio, and then blackness. He knew now what he had been coming to the junkyard to find. He and the others wandering this place were the final occupants of these wrecked automobiles, and their journeys to the afterlife began here. Maybe they all had different circumstances, different stories to reconcile. He knew only that he had come here to confirm his own demise, but more importantly, for one more glimpse of his beloved Elizabeth. She had survived, he was sure of that now, and his relief at that knowledge was immeasurable.

As Michael turned away from the car, he wondered if she yearned for one more moment with him as much as he yearned for her, for one more hug, one more smile. The image of her sitting by the side of the road, disheveled and clearly in shock, had dissolved in his memory into an image of beauty and grace and happiness, his mind able to summon a collection of pictures from the archives of his time with her: her most dazzling smile, her proudest moment, that look of quiet contentment that had become a well of goodness that sustained him during his every waking moment. All of those memories, Elizabeth at her very best, combined into a single image that was almost too much for him to contemplate, like a light too bright to be stared at directly. That was the image that he gathered in his mind, and latched onto for what he was sure was going to be eternity.

He headed back toward the office, his time at the junkyard clearly finished. It was time to move on.

THE WALK

Mieke Zamora–Mackay

The sliding glass doors open and I push my walker through the whooshing air curtain and over the threshold. It's like passing through an invisible wall. On this side, I smell nothing. Yes, nothing has a smell and it's different from the green plants and smog outside. It's the empty scent of an air-freshener disguising decay, death, and urine, but I know it's here.

Seeing me, James stands quickly and fiddles with his collar. He smoothens back his sparse white hair. His bright smile beckons.

Oh, that smile. I first saw it in the summer of 1950, as he stood at the bottom of the steps of City Hall with my cousin, Henry. They were about to board the warship bound for Korea and wanted to enjoy their last night in the city by going out dancing. James was short and stocky then, with a strong sharp chin that jutted over the collar of his white uniform. He wore his jet-black hair slicked back, and liked to smooth it with his hands and a fine-toothed comb. He impressed me with his jolly sense of humor and fancy dancing feet.

"Welcome back, Mother!" James bellows with his arms open wide. My heart is weary of this. I come back every day, hobbling with this creaky, metal stand with tennis balls for feet, hoping that today he'll remember me -- his wife.

Fifty-seven years, God damn it! I immediately cross myself for using the Lord's name in vain. I might as well turn around and go home, but turning with this wretched thing is actually more work than just going forward and getting on with it.

So I smile and play along.

He takes me in his arms and squeezes me instead of hugs. He smells of bleach. He puts his lips to my cheek and sniffs, leaving behind some moisture. I swipe it off with my hand. When he returned from the war, his embraces and kisses left me weak in the knees and wanting. Now, they just hurt from arthritis.

"I am so glad you're here, Mother," James says as he squeezes my arms.

"Henry?" He says to his nursing aide, whose name is Art. "You remember my mother, Joan?"

"Hello Clara," Art says softly with a nod. I wave my hand, dismissing the introduction. He knows I'm playing along, but he never does. All this time, he stands there, as still as a statue.

James picks up my withered hand, and hooks it in the crook of his elbow. He doesn't seem to notice the spots and scabs around my knuckles when he rubs them with his thumb as we walk along the hallway to the social hall. We walked down the aisle to a slow ballad on our wedding day, and I almost ran down it to get to the altar. There's nothing playing now.

I inch forward slowly, pushing the walker with one hand; afraid I might fall if we go any faster. *What's the rush? We're no longer heading home to share a bed!*

The statue follows us silently.

"I have someone for you to meet," James says excitedly, just before we arrive at the dining room. He leads me to a table where Helen, another patient at the home, is sitting. She smiles brightly at us. Her hair is curly and white, and her neck is too long, like a giraffe's.

"Mother, this is Clara," James introduces me to the giraffe. "She's agreed to be my wife." These are the same words he said when I met the real Joan the first time. I bet I didn't look like a giraffe then.

I want to leave, but the statue is standing right behind me. I can't turn. I'm trapped. I let go of James' arm and grip on to the handles of my walker. I feel like crying but don't. They might think them tears of joy. There's pain in my heart, but I know it's not a heart attack. I've had one of those; it didn't hurt nearly as much as this.

I clench my jaw, and force myself to keep steady. I realize now, that I could have my escape. Maybe I don't have to come back here anymore? He's replaced me; forgotten me. Now, if I can only manage to forget him.

I'll probably die before that ever happens.

"Hello Clara! It's so nice to finally meet you," I say to the giraffe and reach out to shake her hand.

Maybe tomorrow, this walk will be different.

WHAT OF CHRISTMAS DREAMS?

Robert Cook

Frank had been sitting on the bench for an hour; his knees were aching, and his right foot had lost all its feeling. He had watched the crowds coming and going from store to store, and milling about the huge Christmas tree that dominated the mall atrium. Around it were brightly wrapped, oversized packages, finished off with ribbons and large bows in various colors. All of them were nestled in billowing cotton-snow, making for a wintery scene in the warmth of the mall.

He gave into the rapidly increasing pains in his knees. He pushed himself off the bench with one hand on the seat, the other hand seizing his cane for support. He struggled for several seconds, nearly falling back onto the bench, but was finally able to stand, tottering precariously. That right foot refused to feel the floor. He steadied himself using his cane, waiting for the tingling ache to stop as his foot woke up.

He wanted to get a closer look at the tree and everything that was going on around it. He took determined yet faltering steps toward the crowd-barrier made up of huge candy canes and gold-flecked ropes. Finally he reached the barrier, and placed one hand on a large candy cane for support.

He stood hunched over, exhausted from the short walk. There was a long queue of children and their parents slowly inching forward. A train chugged and clanged its way around the tree. In front of it all, was the mall's personification of the great man from the North Pole. Santa was seated in his rightful place, a throne backed up against a cotton snowbank.

His head swam with the tragedy and triumph playing out before him: the children being pushed and shoved, urged to be quiet, noses wiped, until they were finally offered up like so many sacrifices to the bearded gentleman. Once they were settled on his knee, they were supposed to unburden themselves of their dreamed-for bounty. For some, it was an opportunity to speak to the "great man;" for others it was a frightening experience— being thrust into the clutches of a stranger, a bearded monster in odd clothes, with a rumbling "Ho Ho Ho" that drove them to scream and kick until they were at last freed, and dragged away by red-faced parents.

His attention shifted across the atrium to a tall, buxom woman in a tight blue sweater and black stretch pants struggling with several large red and green shopping bags—his daughter Janet. She had left him to cool his heels on that hard bench an hour before. He knew that she was searching for him. He was sure that was the case as he watched her continue to look first one way and then another. He thought of waving to get her attention, but gave that up as a bad idea since the effort could easily unbalance him. He wasn't all that sure he wanted to hear the diatribe he knew was coming once she found him. Finally, she spotted him. Her face first showed relief, and then he saw her jaw clench as her anger won out.

She walked quickly up to him. "I told you to stay put. I didn't want you wondering off again. God knows, I don't know what possesses you sometimes!"

He wanted to tell her not to get her pantyhose in a knot, but didn't. He only said, "I was right here. I just wanted to get a closer look."

"Dad! I couldn't find you," she said with a testy whine.

"Look at it, Jan. Isn't it magnificent?"

"What?"

"The tree...the decorations...and look, a train running around it."

"Yeah, pretty nice. Let's go."

Frank knew it was no good to try to convince her that this was something special. He pulled himself erect, up to his full height of six feet, four inches, towering over her. He swayed for a moment, got his bearings, rapped his cane twice on the floor and stepped out. "Let's get a move on it, Jan."

Janet moved up to his unsupported side, shifted her bags to one side, and took his arm. They slowly, laboriously, walked together towards the mall exit. He occasionally took a misstep, lurching to the side, but managed to recover without dragging her with him.

"Take it slow, Dad. There's no rush. We're almost there."

He didn't reply, concentrating on placing one foot in front of the other until they finally made it to the car. She opened the door for him and stood by as he plopped down in the front passenger seat.

"Okay, Dad?"

"Yup. All here, all buckled up. Get me home."

When they were back at the house, he made his way to his favorite chair and let himself down none too gracefully. He gave a sigh of relief, and soon nodded off.

He awoke to the clatter of pots announcing that Janet had delayed her departure.

"You making dinner?"

"Yeah. Don't you remember? The boys are visiting tonight."

Oh, yeah. He looked around the living room and thought of the mall Santa, and the tree.

"Janet?" He waited for a response. Not getting one, he repeated, "Janet!"

"Yeah, Dad?" He heard the sound of her knife chopping something.

"That was quite a tree, wasn't it?"

"Mmmmm."

"Remember when we had a big tree over there in the corner? That was when you and your brother were still home."

"Yeah, Dad."

"David was the first to leave. Then you ran off and got married. Your mother said it was a waste of good money to have a big tree in an empty house. You were starting your own family. You had said that you wanted to create your own traditions."

"What's that, Dad?"

He gave up on the conversation, but continued his musing. "Of course, you wouldn't remember that. You weren't here for the holidays anymore. Do you have any idea what it was like to

103

go to your house and watch your four boys creating joyous mayhem every Christmas? All that ... and then come home to ... to nothing?"

"Yeah, Dad."

"Such joy at your home, then days, weeks, and even months of dreary existence as we waited for the next invitation. Your mother never wanted you to hear a word of complaint about it from me. Then she got sick. Even then, you didn't come around. Too busy, I guess."

"What's that, Dad? Busy? We're always busy."

"Your mother ran a tight ship when you and David were here. Our days weren't our own bringing you guys up."

"Right, Dad."

He stopped speaking aloud, but his thoughts continued. *It wasn't until I retired that it seemed that I had to account for every minute of the day,* he thought. *Without the two of you around, Hannah concentrated on controlling me. Just about every plan I made or suggested was immediately vetoed by her as being impractical, too expensive, or just plain stupid. It got worse as time went on, and her health began to fail. Do you know what drives me crazy? You're just like your mother.*

It has only been a month since I followed that double line of six men. The travel forward over the mucky ground had come to a halt, two more steps and I nearly bumped into the end of that line. I had been distracted. I had been remembering times past; other walks across that same lawn, other double lines struggling to keep their footing over the uneven ground.

She was no longer there. She could no longer veto the things he wanted to do. It wasn't as if those things were extravagant. But, the years had mounted up, and he wanted to make a change before it was too late. He needed to hear the joy of young children around him in his own house, the gratification of seeing a happy family.

His reverie was interrupted with the arrival of his grandsons. The noise of four boisterous young men, who thought nothing of beating on one another for the slightest provocation, rolled over him like a warm summer wave. After dinner they gathered in the living room.

"You know, boys, when your mother and Uncle Dave were young we always had a big tree ... a live one."

Janet yelled from the kitchen, "Live trees? Hah. You remember those aluminum jobs with the light that rotated with different colors?"

He heard only part of what she had said. He continued, "I remember most Christmases we gave big parties. Your grandmother loved big parties. There was so much excitement. I can tell you, so many of those parties seemed to go on for most of the night. It was always an effort to shoo everyone home by three in the morning so we could prepare for the big day."

He saw Janet hovering in the background, a grim visage on her face, her eyes rolling towards the ceiling as she was preparing to leave.

"We always let your mother and Uncle Dave open a present on Christmas Eve. It was our way of encouraging them to go to bed early. There was only one present under the tree on the Eve. Santa brought the rest during the night."

He saw their grins as he talked. He wondered if they were imagining the wonders of the Christmases he described.

"Boys, you should have seen the train going around that tree at the mall. Wouldn't it be wonderful if I could get a tree? I'd put it in that corner. There'd be a train that chugged and clanged its way around it carrying miniature packages." He paused for several seconds. "But, buying all that would mean I'd have to make another trek to the mall. I'm not up to doing that any time soon."

As the last words exited his mouth, he was sure that there were probably some dreams that would never be fulfilled. But what were dreams good for if you couldn't hope.

Janet said, "It's impractical. Besides, what would you do with it?"

He cringed every time she repeated words that Hannah would have used. He thought he saw some conspiratorial glances between the boys. Or perhaps it was just a reaction to their mother's words.

Several days later, unexpectedly, a tree—a six and a half foot tree, with more lights than he could imagine—appeared, coming through his door with the assistance of Matt and his brother Jamie. They quickly had it erected in the corner of the living room, and decorated. The tree was everything he had hoped for. The lights were dazzling. Frank was grateful, and sat long after the boys left, reflecting in the glow of the lights and dozed off with the imagined sound of a train circling below.

As the days sped by with alarming rapidity towards Christmas, wrapped parcels appeared from various family members and lovingly placed under the tree. Frank would sit in his chair in the late evening marveling at the tree, and the ever-increasing gaily wrapped packages beneath it.

Christmas Eve found him at Janet's for the family's Christmas party. It was his first without Hannah, one of many firsts of doing things without her. When the evening finally wound down, and most of the relatives had departed, Janet drove him home. She sat with him for a few minutes in the living room, taking in the lights of the tree and the colorful packages beneath. Then she said she had to return home, and was quickly out the door. The day had been strenuous, taking its toll on him. He turned off the lights and retired to his bed.

He awoke at midnight, and watched as the bright red numerals of the alarm clock clicked over to 12:01. He said to the empty room, "Happy Christmas to me."

He put on his slippers and shuffled into the living room. He had to remind himself there was no need to be quiet, after all, he didn't have to worry about waking Hannah. It just seemed like the thing to do. Old habits were hard to break.

He turned on the tree lights, and sat in his chair taking it all in. He was feeling a sense of what family meant with all the wonderful things everyone had been doing for him. And the star, placed at the top of the tree, reminded him of that first nativity. It all made his heart glow with peace and thankfulness. He turned off the lights and returned to bed, easily falling asleep again with dreams of Christmas trees, Santa Claus, and the small baby in a manger filling his sleeping mind.

In the morning, he prepared to make the trek to Church for the Christmas Mass. When he walked into the living room, he was surprised to see the tree lights were on, and there was somehing else, a sound...a new sound...the sound of a train making its chugging, clanging way around the tree. He nearly fell over from surprise, just managing to reach his chair before collapsing into it--watching the train going round and round through the tears that had welled up and were coursing down his cheeks. For ten minutes, Frank sat there in wonder.

He finally gathered himself together, not wanting to be late for the Christmas mass. When he opened the door, he was faced with a crowd of his children, grandchildren, and great-grandchildren. Everyone pressed forward to hug and kiss him, nearly knocking him over in their enthusiasm to wish him a Merry Christmas. Matt put his arm around his grandfather's shoulder, and whispered, "How about that train?" and smiled. He looked at his eldest grandson to express his thanks, but all he could do was smile. Janet helped him into his car, while everyone else piled into their waiting cars to make the short trip to church. He looked at Janet as she was driving. He saw a grin beginning to form on her lips.

She looked quickly at him and said, "What?" in that whining voice she used all too often.

Once more, he said nothing, only smiled.

All through the service, Frank listened to the message of the mass, while in the back of his mind were the sounds of a train chugging and clanging around his tree. Sometimes dreams do come true.

BAD DAY FOR SANTA

John Farquhar

I was eight years old, and having an honest, innocent pee in a public toilet when Santa Claus came in. I didn't notice him at first. When I pee, then as now, I look down. I was aware of a large adult figure sidling up to the urinal beside me. I didn't turn my head. As soon as his pee started, mine stopped. There's a word for this condition, which runs in my family, that for the life of me, I can't remember. I looked up in frustration and saw his jolly, fat red face. I couldn't believe my luck.

"Santa!" I gasped.

"Hey kid!" said Santa.

I, and no doubt he, was not used to talking to strangers in public toilets, so an awkward silence fell. I broke it with the first thought that came into my head:

"You pee!"

"Sure I pee. I'm only human."

"You're only human?!"

Santa smiled, frowned, and a light sweat appeared upon his brow.

"I'm mostly human, I mean. Human, 'cos, like you, I drink; and, after I drink, I pee. It's normal. Everyone pees."

"God doesn't."

"No. No, He don't. I never said He did."

"God doesn't pee, I said, proudly, "because he doesn't have a body."

"No. No, he don't."

"He doesn't drink because he never gets thirsty and so, he never pees."

"Is that what they teach you in school these days?"

"No, I worked it out for myself."

"Good for you."

"Dead people don't pee either," I went on.

"I suppose not."

Santa's stream, I noticed, has suddenly stopped. Not a tinkle.

"Do you give presents to dead people?" I continued brightly. It was something I'd wanted to know for a while, but never had the courage to ask.

"Do I what?!"

"Do you give presents to dead people?"

"No."

"Why not?"

"They're dead!"

"So?"

I wasn't angry, just excited. I think Santa thought I was angry, because he said, quite sharply:

"How old are you, anyway, kid?"

"Eight."

"Eight. You're eight years old. It's Christmas. You've just met Santa, and all you can talk about is pee and dead people. You need to loosen up, kid."

"Other people sometimes tell me that," I replied. "I don't think they understand. I'm just curious."

"You said it. Anyway, Merry Christmas!"

"Merry Christmas, Santa."

Santa zipped up and, with an old guy's groan, moved away. I turned around to watch him go. Perhaps I shouldn't have turned around, because he did a very bad thing which had terrible consequences for both of us. Having just had a pee, Santa did something unforgivable:

HE DIDN'T WASH HIS HANDS.

He wiped them a little, on his tunic, but I knew that didn't count. I couldn't believe my eyes. I zipped up and stood in the middle of the bathroom, about to call him back. It was too late. He had opened the door. Outside, in the mall, four elves were waiting to escort him back to the Grotto. Behind the elves stood my mother. She saw me and smiled as the door swung shut again. He was gone, with germs on his hands.

"Oh my God!" I said. "Oh, my God! Oh, my God!"

I washed and rinsed my hands for thirty seconds in lukewarm water, looking at my pale reflection in the mirror. Avoiding the unsanitary towel, I dried my hands electronically, and shuffled towards the door. I didn't want to go out, but my mother knocked on the door and called my name, so I had to.

"Well!" She said, a big smile on her face.

"Well?" I replied.

"Did you speak to him?"

"Who?"

"Who?! Santa of course!"

"I guess."

"You guess? What's wrong?"

"Nothing."

"Oh yes, there is. What is it?"

"I don't want to say."

My mother was getting worried.

"Well, you need to. What's the matter?"

Looking into her eyes, I felt an overwhelming need to tell her everything, and nothing. I looked down, shuffled my feet and said:

"Santa did a bad thing in there."

All the maternal hormones in my mother's body pulsed into her brain, causing her face to collapse.

"Oh my God! Oh, my God! He did a bad...thing...to you?"

"No."

My mother's face was restored, but only for a moment.

"Oh my God, you mean...he did a bad thing...to himself?"

"Sort of."

"What did he do?"

"I don't want to say."

"You need to tell me."

"I don't want to get Santa into trouble."

"If Santa did something bad, I need to know. Anyway, he's not the real Santa."

"He's not?"

"No. He's a store Santa. They're different."

"How?"

"They help Santa for a few weeks every Christmas. There are lots of them. They're not magic, like the real Santa."

"He's not magic," I repeated, relieved. "I knew it! That's why he has to pee!"

"What?"

"The real Santa is magic, and doesn't pee. The same as God, and dead people."

My mother looked upwards, and seemed to say a little prayer to someone. Then she continued, remorselessly:

"So...what *did* he do in there?"

"I don't want..."

"Tell me!"

"He..."

"He what?"

"He didn't..."

"Didn't WHAT?"

"He didn't wash his hands."

I covered my face in my hands, then looked up at my mother. I was a hero and a coward at the same time. My mother nodded for a while, said "men!" very softly under her breath, then turned around to the Grotto, where Santa had a baby on his knee. The baby was crying, and Santa was trying his best to wipe away its tears with his thumb; the tears made his thumb wet, and he dried it, on his tunic.

"Oh, my God!" My mother said. "That's disgusting! Disgusting. I'm going to complain!"

"No, don't!" I shouted, alarmed.

My mother stormed off towards the Complaints Department which, as chance would have it, was opposite the Grotto. I waved at Santa, pointed desperately towards my mother, made a sign that he was about to get his neck cut off, and tried to show him in sign language that it really wasn't my fault. Santa, having given back the baby, saw me, but didn't seem to get it, so I repeated every gesture. He gazed blankly at me, then gave a start, as a large toddler was dropped into his lap.

I edged towards the Complaints Department, and, in helpless fascination, watched the tragedy unfold: my mother told the assistant; the assistant tut-tutted and phoned the manager; the manager appeared, shook his head remorsefully, and gave my mother a book of coupons. Then, he strode over to the Grotto, with a "Closed" sign under his arm.

The next thing I knew, Santa was being escorted out of the mall by four security guards. A sign had been put up by the Grotto saying Santa had had to leave early today, but that he would be back tomorrow. The elves looked stunned. The children in the queue cried in disappointment, until they were allowed to help themselves to anything they wanted from Santa's sack.

I poured things over in my mind: Santa had done a bad thing, and now he had to pay. I understood that much, but I could see he wasn't all bad, and that he really needed a friend at this difficult time, so I walked with Santa and his escort for a while, until he glared at me.

"Are you going to wash your hands now, Santa?" I asked.

"No, I'm not. I've been let go."

"But, at least you'll be back tomorrow?"

"Santa will. Not me. Someone else. I'll never be Santa again."

I decided to try to explain:

"I didn't mean it, Santa," I said.

"Mean what?"

"I...accidentally told my mom that you forgot to wash your hands."

Santa stopped. The four security guards stopped and one of them gently tugged his arm. Santa looked deep into my eyes. I'll never forget the final words he spoke to me, words which, from that time onwards, I've always associated with Christmas:

"Thanks a lot, kid. Now how the fuck am I gonna pay the rent?"

FOOTPRINTS THAT DON'T MATCH

Dawn Byrne

Royal blue sculptured wall-to-wall carpet. This fantastic tint is better fit for play than décor, with surrounding golden walls our undying sun. The carpet's visible texture is little rippling waves. We sail along. Our vessel is Grandma's Early American seaworthy sofa. When our baby brother climbs aboard, we spring a leak and all five of us abandon ship.

*

A fog rises outside our front door from our car that's under the weather. Grandma teeters through the smoke that mixes with real rain. It's slippery for Grandma to get up the slick front steps. But a dark cloud in our living room ceiling finally got too heavy from the bathtub leaking, so she had to go to the hardware store for an elbow pipe that doesn't bend.

Grandma comes into the house limping over the carpet leaving damp footprints that don't match; one print is wider than the other because her real foot got bigger but the artificial one didn't.

My sister struts from side to side carrying the elbow, mimicking Grandma behind her wide back. I never tried crossing the ocean like that before. My sister walks a gait of faith; if Grandma sees her she'll be damned. I'll try my strut after Grandma swims upstairs along the continuous blue carpet that flows upstream.

My sister gives me the elbow and disappears. Grandma's now swimming her special stroke, bobbing to catch a breath every few feet. Our grandma is like God. She's huge and strong and old and

115

alive. Dad's not. He's in a silk box with his head shaved, sleeping from cancer. I remember him lying there so still. I don't remember him walking on the water much when he wasn't sleeping.

I feel bad for Rosa. She's my friend who sits next to me in class. Her dad didn't get sick; he got mean. He doesn't live with her anymore. He's not in Heaven though. Rosa and her mom moved into her grandma's house. If Rosa's dad moves into her grandma's house too, maybe he will be in Heaven.

Grandma just swam over the horizon. I'll try to do it. Back up against the far wall, between the two front windows with my heels touching the baseboards. Take a deep breath. Maybe I'll close my eyes.

Uh-oh, Grandma's calling me. I'll have to paddle upstream fast.

"Go downstairs and get the wrench from my pocketbook. It's beside my chair," Grandma calls from under the bathtub when I hand her the elbow. The front of her dress is wet and her artificial leg is standing beside the toilet. The leg's metal like the pipe, but it does bend and if it gets wet, it'll rust. I go downstairs and look for the wrench.

Back upstairs, I pant, "Grandma, it's not in your pocketbook."

"It has to be. Look again."

I look again.

"Grandma, I looked real hard and it's not there. Just the hammer." Now I'm breathing hard.

"Well then it has to be in the tool box in the cellar."

After swimming downstream again and hopping down rocks that are the cellar steps, I look for the wrench, praying it's there. Yep!

"Here you go Grandma." I beam, dripping like I really did go swimming.

She curses. "The spigot's leaking back here too." Grandma takes the wrench. "Go down in the cellar, on the shelf, under the stairs. There's a small baby food jar with washers in it. Bring me up one."

*

The ocean is now a football field. Furniture and toys crowd along one side of the living and dining room thoroughfare. The TV and more toys cheer us on along the opposite side. Our team runs from the kitchen's back door straight through the house to the front door and greets visiting players. The fifty-yard line is marked by a fraying hole. No one knows who made it. Or who dropped the gum that's now a flat black circle on our thirty-yard line.

Many long, hard games are played here. Grandma referees in her striped dress that looks like the rest of her wardrobe; A-line (I don't know why they call dresses A-line) with no sleeves. She made them all herself. She has the patience of a saint.

"Jesus, Mary and Joseph! Stop running in the house. And close the god damn door. You weren't born in a barn," Grandma yells to my brother Dan. She stops him at the sixty-yard line.

"But Grandma there's still more wood at the curb that Joe from the shop next-door said I can have," says Dan.

Grandma fouls his hoarding. "There's enough wood in that yard as it is. We'll have a firetrap back there soon."

"Please Grandma, the trash truck's comin'?"

She shakes her head. Dan breaks away and makes it to the twenty-yard line as the truck roars up our block.

Grandma forgot the leg upstairs so she uses a crutch to penalize our offending player. In mid-air the yellow flag crutch becomes a harpoon and we are back on a calm ocean.

*

The stairs are a pier now. We dangle Grandma's crocheting yarn from it. We have fun casting it from her crocheting hook and pretending to reel in a big catch.

We're fine sports, but Grandma isn't because the store doesn't sell that color yarn anymore.

The pier disappears and we're rowing upstream, dodging harpoons and One-legged Pete. Tonight we also sport tanned hides. Onto The Old West.

In the morning we're herded from our corrals beyond the stairs' horizon, through the blue grass carpet to where we're fed. Grandma nips at our heels so we'll hurry. She growls when my sister reaches for the TV. Those pastures are forbidden; it's a school day. But Grandma has a date with John Wayne at 1 pm. I watched him last week when I was home from school, sick. He walks funny as he approaches his horse, like he used Grandma's yarn for a lasso. He'll just be riding into the sunset when we come home.

We learned in Sunday School that God has different names; Jehovah, Yahweh, Alpha and Omega. Grandma does too. She gave my mom a different last name than she has, and my uncle an even different one than those. Goodness knows how many others she has. Could Wayne be one? When I ask her about them, Grandma always needs me to do something for her, so I stopped asking.

*

I don't know why Grandma gets upset when the neighbors ask questions about our family. I like our neighbors. They're so friendly and concerned about us.

From our kitchen snack bar I see Mrs. Rudner looking at me. She's peeping out her sun porch window which is across our street. I don't wave to her because she may think I'm staring at her and that's rude.

The other day she asked me if our dryer was broken because she saw Grandma hanging laundry in our back yard (I hope Grandma remembered not to wave). When I told her we didn't have a dryer, she made that tsk-tsk sound with her tongue and mumbled, "...with five children in that house."

I assured her that we had a washing machine, but that I'm not allowed to help with the laundry because my mom got her finger stuck in the rollers when she was my age. Mrs. Rudner just stared at me with her mouth open.

I heard our next-door neighbor say to her neighbor how awful it is when Ms. Gimpy says "GD" all the time right in front of her grandkids. From the way they whispered, that must be worse than a four-letter word. When I asked Grandma who Ms. Gimpy is, she says, "Those god damned gossips should mind their own business."

*

"Grandma, can I play with this?" my brother asks.

"Where'd you get that from?" Grandma barks.

"He was rooting around behind your chair," my sister tattles

"What is it?" I ask.

"That's my Bingo dabber," Grandma says.

"Can I see it?" my sister dares.

"No, put it back in my Bingo bag right now."

"Are you going to Bingo at OLPH, Grandma?" I ask.

"Yeah. Now get that from your brother before he gets it all over...Jesus Christ!"

We tease my brother about being the Blue Boy, like the picture hanging in our hallway upstairs. He snickers as we watch Grandma lug her Bingo bag and huge pocketbook into her friend's car. Her blue eye shadow almost matches my brother's hands.

Grandma has lots of friends at Bingo, including the priest. They're glad to see her come, and even pick her up when our car isn't running. I don't know why she can't take communion on Sunday mornings at OLPH. I guess because we're Protestant. That means you go to a smaller church when your car is running and drink watery grape juice.

*

"Jesus, Mary and Joseph!..............Ass...Sh..." Grandma's talking to the nativity again. As I walk into our house after school, I hear her voice coming from the open cellar door. Tip-toeing to the TV set, I turn on Speed Racer.

"Dawn Marie! Get your nose out of that TV and do your homework." Grandma's no longer talking to clay figures.

My stomach hurts and the back of my neck feels funny when I hear the muffled thud of Grandma's artificial leg on the bottom step. My body jumps and I grab my school bag. I'm sure she's coming because of more thuds. Time is running out. The thuds are louder, closer. I scramble to get out my loose leaf book and flip to spelling. The thuds stop. I hear breathing. I feel her standing there but can't look up from my list of words. She coughs her familiar cigarette cough and says, "Hand me your spelling words."

119

I hate spelling. I hate Thursdays because every Friday my teacher gives us a spelling test. Grandma makes me study right after school. She says to just do it and get it over with.

"Spell 'receive'."

"R-E-C-I-E-V-E."

"Try it again."

"R-E-C...E-I-V-E."

"Spell 'conquest'."

"C-O-N-Q-U-I-S-T."

"No."

"I studied. Honest, but I can't get 'em right."

"You got most of 'em. Conquest."

"I can't get them last ones."

"Yes you can. Medicine."

"M-E-D-I-C-I-N."

Grandma stares at the list. "Am I right?" I ask, but Grandma's still quiet, leaning her ear at me. "E."

"Good. Now listen, conqu..e...st."

"C-O-N-Q-U-E-S-T."

Grandma gives me back the list and says, "You got 'em all."

"Shouldn't I try it one more time just to make sure? I don't wanna get one of those hard ones wrong."

"You're done. Go play."

*

We're on vacation at the real ocean. Grandma teases us about sharks so we don't go out too far: "Damn things swim faster'n a man. Can swallow 'em whole too."

We meet a kid who plays in our half of the beach house the whole week we're here. We don't know his name. He just shows up, even when we don't want him to. Grandma serves us Kool-Aide. She drinks iced tea with no sugar, and has to take off her artificial leg when it gets too hot for her to wear it.

The day we go home, we say good-bye to the kid we're hoping came with the house we're now leaving. He takes a good, long look at Grandma and says, "Hey! You ain't got no teeth." Grandma laughs her hardy laugh that comes from deep down in her big belly and struts into the bedroom to check for stuff we forgot. She has us each grab a bag or box to take to the car.

I feel bad for the kid because he isn't one of us. He's different, like one of those kids who have their own bedroom. I bet he's scared at night all by himself.

I think he's gonna cry standing in the corner of the living room watching us. You can tell he wants to come along because his body leans side-to-side as we come back for more stuff and go out again.

The car's packed and Dan whispers, "Hey Grandma, that boy's still here. Is he comin' with us?"

The kid's feet don't move until Grandma says, "You're gonna have to go home now."

He looks at Grandma and the rest of us like our dog looks at my brother when he's leaving to go to school in the morning. That's how I'd look if I were him. He doesn't say anything and runs away fast.

HOLD ON TIL THE END

Jennifer M. Eaton

The last of my strength wanes as the wind kicks up once more. My grasp slips as I hang, pummeled by the slapping severity of nature, mocking my fate. The last of my sisters falls, the wind taking her spiraling to places unbeknownst to all.

The storm subsides, and I grieve over the loss of my siblings. Our home, naked and ravaged, stark among the growing sunlight, stands firm—whole, but somehow less. Empty.

Exhausted, I let go, and spiral down into the unknown. Life, need, the desire to hang on—fleeting and gone. A light breeze catches me, and slows my descent, until I lay quietly and comfortably below the great cherry tree, cradled in the soft embrace of my sister petals who fell before me.

RADIANCE

Christine L. Hardy

The light is there, warm and golden
Just beyond my reach
Shaded by the edge of consciousness
It filters through thoughts and flesh
Tangled regrets, fears, sorrows binding
Pulling me back into the reek
Of humanity

Oh, don't slip behind a cloud now!
Hide not your face from me
Let me see it just once unveiled
Shine upon me like glass
Through which the sun's rays
Show each imperfection
In gilded radiance

WHERE ARE YOU ZEPPIE?

Or: The Hazards of Caring for Virtual Dependents

Marie Gilbert

I have nine grandchildren, six who live nearby. I was asked to babysit my grandsons when my daughter and son-in-law went on a second honeymoon. The boys are usually great with me, but on the second night of watching them, I had to play the part of Judge Judy and designate who was going to play a video game on the large flat screen TV. I chose the 17-year-old as the winner, and his brothers and I called it a night.

I awoke very late in the night to hear the 17-year-old yelling. What was Jimmy yelling at? I found him in front of the T.V. carrying on a conversation.

"Who are you talking to?" I asked, curious since it was only the two of us in the room.

"Dominic," he replied, his attention riveted to the screen as the characters in his video game flashed and bombed and exploded.

"Okay..." I replied, wondering if I should call his parents to inform them their eldest was speaking to the television.

"Dominic said hello," my grandson informed me.

"He can see me through the TV?" I asked as I waved at the screen.

"Oh my God," he replied with a good natured laugh as he told his friend what I was doing. He then turned around to show me the headset he was wearing. After patiently explaining how he was simultaneously playing this game with several of his friends, I made my way back to bed feeling quite sorry for myself.

I'm a geek at heart, but sadly, I'm what the young kids call "technology challenged."

The next day, the two younger boys were playing a video game called the Legend of Zelda, The Twilight Princess. I had heard of the game, but this was the first time I watched anyone play, so I asked questions.

"Who kidnapped her? Does Link get to marry her when he saves her? Can you talk to your friends on the T.V. when you're playing this game?" I was curious, since I knew the game had been around a long time. But their expressions of disbelief confirmed last night's feelings. I left the room feeling like a dinosaur and in need of a cup of tea.

This brings me to Zeppie, my Webkin puppy. A few years ago, the youngest grandson asked me to buy myself a Webkin. Webkins are plush toys that have a virtual interactive image on the webkin site. Nathan wanted my Webkin puppy to send *his* Webkin puppy e-mails and gifts. I did what any grandmother would do for a grandchild, and bought myself a Webkin puppy.

What he failed to tell me was I had to take care of this puppy on the internet. Not only was I forced to buy furniture and sign Zeppie up for after school projects, but I had to do farming to feed him. If I failed to keep the puppy well fed and entertained, I was called into the Doctor's office. It's really embarrassing to have a cartoon doctor tell you that your cartoon puppy is sick.

But days would pass and because I was busy in real life, my imaginary plants would die. It is a lot of work to care for a virtual farm. You have to click and scroll a rake to each plant, plus water and nurse the farm back to health, on each return. On top of this constant worry, my oldest granddaughter, who was in college at the time, asked me to join her vampire group on Facebook. Did I really want to do this? Not really, but I am an obedient grandmother. I adopted a vampire.

To keep my virtual bloodsucker alive, I had to fight zombies, werewolves and other vampires to move up the ranks. I had to send out requests to my Facebook friends to please allow me to bite their necks. If they agreed, I would earn more points. But only a few did, probably thinking me a little strange. To find the time to care for both of my online dependents, I tried to figure out how to use the vampires to do the farming for Zeppie. It didn't work.

Busy with work, I visited my virtual dependents less and less to rake or battle. One day, I logged in, but Zeppie didn't appear. I had no idea what had happened, but he didn't appear the next time either. And God only knows where my Level 6 vampire went to. She had vanished from my Facebook page. I was crushed over losing the two of them.

So now I hope that my Facebook friends don't take it personally when I won't help them with Farmville and refuse those other game requests. I'm having major guilt trips as it is, although NOT having virtual dependents gives me more time to spend with real people. I guess all I can hope for is that Zeppie is happy in Webkin heaven and that my female vampire got a bit part on *True Blood* and is doing well.

Barbara Godshalk

DRIVING LESSONS

Barbara Godshalk

Putting it mildly, I was a late bloomer. Growing up in Philadelphia, I had no urgent desire for a car as I approached my teen years. Public transportation was pervasive and the only need I had for a license was for proof of age to get into nightclubs. As my twenty-first birthday approached, my father contacted Sears. Watch for the antique reference: a dual-control Chrysler K-car pulled up to our house and off we went.

I do not remember much about the instructor or the bulk of the lessons. What I do remember, however, was him directing me onto Interstate 95. He kept telling me to breathe. There were probably hand impressions from my death grip on the steering wheel. I never did get a car when we lived in the city. About a year later, my parents decided to move to southern New Jersey.

Learning to drive to pass your driver's test is vastly different, of course, from finding your destination without wrinkling your car or "making new friends." One would think that learning to drive in New Jersey, a state famous for its drivers, would be "exciting," to say the least. Ironically, and luckily, it turned out to be largely uneventful.

Over the years, I ran into the occasional obnoxious boob behind the wheel but mercifully nothing ever really happened outside of the exchange of fingers. That was as common as crabgrass. It made me wonder how New Jersey got such a bad reputation until...

My husband and I decided to take a trip to Cape Cod before we started our family. We Googled directions to an amazing-bed and-breakfast in Centerville, Massachusetts. The trip was supposed to take somewhere around seven hours by car, and we were up for it. So we packed up the "Orolla" and set off. (The "C" had fallen off of Dave's Toyota several months earlier and we had no clue where it was.)

We started up the New Jersey Turnpike and were making pretty good time. As we got closer to the Jersey side of New York City, they appeared. By "they," I mean the New Jersey single members of team "Up Yours." My husband was driving and bravely fought off the tailgating, getting cut off repeatedly, and navigating unfamiliar territory. Thankfully, our daughter was just a plan at that point so foul language was not an issue.

It's always a shock whenever I leave my own little corner of Small Town, New Jersey and venture up to the northern part of the state. The major metropolitan area syndrome seems to spread beyond the over-caffeinated city limits, thus extending the size of the potential manic driving area beyond the actual borders.

What was funny, at least to me, as a passenger, was that once we survived passing through Northern New Jersey and New York City, we thought the worst was over. Wrong!

When we entered Massachusetts we encountered some drivers who made the Jersey devils look polite! More often than not the "offenders" were driving what we like to call "FUVs," but there were plenty of other types of cars, too.

We've often joked about how it's amazing we humans survive as a species, since there are obviously some weak members in the herd. But must every damn one of them have a license? What happens to humans when we get behind the wheel? Are we all suddenly in some bad cartoon where everyone else on the road is crazy and extremely late? You could have hugged the stuffing out of every person we met in Massachusetts who was not driving. But put them behind the wheel? Maniacs!

My spouse, God bless him, is the most polite driver I know. "That guy's from out of state, he's probably lost." "Nobody's letting that guy in, I'll wave him over." I asked David who taught him how to drive. "My dad taught me," he said. Something tells me he learned a lot before he ever got in the car.

BEACH MORNING

Robert Cook

The breeze coming in the window off the bay the night before had been chill, making me gather up the cotton blanket beneath my chin as I fell asleep to the sounds of cicadas and the distant surf. It was the early morning light that brought bird song on that same breeze. The sun had not yet warmed my side of the house. I lay there in my warm cocoon, listening. I have no need of alarm clocks; all I knew was that the birds were awake, the sun was up, and it was my hour to rise.

Throwing off the blanket, I searched for the shorts that I had kicked off into a corner the night before. I pulled them on, and padded in bare feet across the cool linoleum floor, feeling the fine grit of sand that seems to be everywhere in the house. Mom was always complaining, "I can't keep ahead of you boys. You've got to wipe your feet before you come in. I'm tired of cleaning up sand every time you traipse through the house. I think there's more sand in here than on the beach—and you brought it all in." This, of course, all fell on deaf ears. How could we keep the sand out? It was everywhere. If we wiped our feet, our shorts still held great repositories of the stuff, ready to be deposited wherever we went. The sand under foot on the linoleum felt...well, it felt as if it belonged there. After all, this was a beach house. What did they expect? I crept into the kitchen and edged open the refrigerator door, looking for orange juice. I pulled a glass from the drain board and poured some for myself.

I walked out to the front porch. The sun was just above the horizon, and already the heat of the day could be felt radiating onto my bare legs, chest, and face. It was going to be a hot one. I could tell. I sat on the steps of the wide wrap-around porch, and listened to the birds. I watched the red-winged blackbirds flit among the reeds across the street. The bright red patch gave them away as they perched and then flew from one reed to another.

The house was still asleep. It was only me and the birds greeting the new day. There was no one about. For several minutes I sat, trying to decide what to do. I looked back into the house through the screen door. The clock on the kitchen wall said it was a quarter to six. Early. The rest of the family wouldn't be up for another hour. I stood, and walked down the steps, out the path, through the gate and turned right. The beach was only a block away.

My feet trod upon the small sand dunes that had formed on the sidewalk next to the grass. It was much more comfortable walking on the loose sand than the concrete sidewalk. I found my way to the beach and stood at the top of a dune, watching the low surf break along the beach. The waves rolled along the jetties, covered the outer ends, moved in on each side of the dark wood pilings until it finally spilled up the beach with an edge of white foam that marked it farthest reach. It then receded, leaving wet sand that changed color as the water soaked in. There were white-breasted sandpipers, their backs a mottled two-tone tan, that raced up and down the beach, keeping just ahead of the water's edge as it came in; and then scampering back out following the wave as it ebbed. Back and forth—back and forth—they searched for some tiny morsel to eat.

The sand was warming under my feet, and I dug in my toes, reaching for the cooler sand several inches below the surface. There were some mornings when I came out here, that wherever I walked in the dunes, there were white patches that showed where I had stepped, following me. Not that day. The morning dew hadn't been enough to darken the sand. Where I walked, there were only soft pockets in the sand that looked like every other indentation. They were all mixed together and gave no clue as to where I had been. There was no way anyone or anything could follow my path, and know where I had been. I was safe.

I walked down to the water's edge and chased the sandpipers. They rose swiftly before me, and then came down again as quickly as I passed. The chill water splashed my legs and splattered my shorts. I walked from the jetty at the end of our street down the expanse of beach towards the next jetty, the distance of a block one from the other. I returned to the dunes and climbed to the top of a wind-blown sand cliff. I jumped down the steep sand wall, landing in soft sugar up to my knees. I climbed the dune and repeated this several more times. Soon, though, I was tired of the long climbing runs. My stomach was telling me it was time for breakfast.

The sand on my wet legs dried as I walked towards the house, and I brush the clinging sand from my legs. On reaching the porch, Mom was standing there.

"Where have you been?" with that look she gave me that said, *don't you dare give me some sassy remark.*

I answered, "Down to the dunes. I watched the sun come up." This wasn't quite the truth, but it was close enough for my Mom's information.

"Well, brush off and get inside. Breakfast will be ready in five minutes. I was just going to send your bother to find you."

"I'm sorry, Mom. I was just down the dunes."

"Okay, get in here...and don't track in any sand. It's too early to be sweeping up after you."

She retreated into the house, the screen door closed with a bang behind her. I stood on the porch, and brushed off more sand. I could smell the bacon frying, and heard the voices of my brother and father. Everyone was up, and preparing for a new day. I swung wide the screen door, hearing the squeak and strain of the long spring. I took several steps into the room, the grit of sand beneath my feet, and the door slammed shut behind me. What a glorious, satisfying sound that was to me. The sound of a wooden screen door slamming is as much a part of being at the beach house as anything else; the birds, the sand, the ocean always beating against the shore.

A new day had begun and I was ready for it. I had had my little piece of beach to myself; my favorite experience, especially on those dewy mornings when the only steps were mine. It was as if I was the first kid on the earth, and the beach was mine.

ACKNOWLEDGEMENTS

This book, and our writers' group, was made possible by the talents and commitment of our members. Specifically, the editors are indebted to:

K.A. Magrowski, for taking the reins of our monthly meetings with timeliness, dedication, and unfailing inspiration;

Janice Wilson, founder of the SJ Writers' Group, for starting something that many of us don't think we can live without;

Robert Cook, for getting this book off the ground and then adding fuel to the fire;

Shelley Szajner, for the outstanding cover design;

James Knipp, for his artful arrangement of the author bios;

Patti O'Brien, for her eagle-eyed edit of the finished manuscript;

Glenn Walker, for his marketing and blog advice, expertise and encouragement;

And all the contributors who so eagerly embraced this project, excitedly inquired after its progress, and enthusiastically offered encouragement. All we can say is: you're right, it WAS a lot of work. Thanks for taking this journey with us!

Amy and Marie

ABOUT THE AUTHORS

Arechavala, Joseph. "Destiny in Dusty Springfield"
Joseph is a 2008 graduate of Rutgers University. He has had poems and stories published in Pearl Magazine, Skyline Magazine, and many others, both online and in print. Joseph's first novel, *Darkness Persists*, has recently been accepted for publication.

Bergeron, Kitty. "Phone Call"
Kitty is a moderator on Literati Revolt, an online community dedicated toward providing critiques and advice to young writers. She is Editor-in-Chief of the LR online magazine, Literati Quarterly. Kitty enjoys writing provocative stories that resonate with the reader. She can be found all over the internet @KittyBergeron.

Byrne, Dawn. "Footprints That Don't Match"
Dawn Byrne is a full-time creative non-fiction writer who enjoys membership in three local writers' groups. She is an event organizer for The South Jersey Writer's Group. Two of her spiritual poems have been published in anthologies. She uses journaling and letter writing as writing tools and for personal inspiration.

Cook, Robert. "Beach Morning," "A Christmas Story"
Bob grew up in Haddonfield, NJ, and resides in Blackwood, NJ with his wife of 37 years. He was a technical writer during his career as an IT Systems Analyst. Upon retirement from corporate America, Bob began to write essays and fiction. He has published a personal essay and was the First Prize winner for Literary Short Fiction at the 2009 Philadelphia Writers' Conference.

Costantino, Joanne. "Leaving the Leaves," "Philly Girl in Jersey" Joanne is a transplanted Philly girl braving the wilds of Washington Township with her husband of 39 years, her grown children, grandchildren, and a Mexican mutt, rescued from the docks of Cozumel, named "Tula." You can read her views about living the life you didn't sign up for at www.joannecostantino.com.

Eaton, Jennifer M. "Hold on 'til the End" Jennifer lives on the East Coast of the USA with her husband, three energetic boys, and a pepped-up poodle. Her greatest joy is using her overactive imagination constructively, creating new worlds for everyone to enjoy. Find more about Jennifer's thoughts and advice as a writer at www.jennifermeaton.com.

Farquhar, John. "Bad Day for Santa" John Farquhar was born in England and educated at Liverpool University and St. John's College, Oxford. He moved to New Jersey with his wife and two daughters seven years ago. He teaches languages and literature at Rutgers University and Temple University. He has had a number of stories published in literary magazines, and a play performed at The Churchill Theatre, Bromley, in England. John is currently marketing a comic novel, *In Search of Grace Devine*, and an indispensable guide to the Next World, *What To Expect When You're Dead.*

Gilbert, Marie. "Where are you, Zeppie?" "Night of the Attack" Marie is a multi-dimensional super-heroine with more adventures than a comic book museum, stuck in a grandmother's body. She grew up in a large Italian family who loved to tell stories of all kinds, which sparked her lifelong love of writing. After retiring from the Academy of Natural Sciences in Philadelphia, she finally had time to work on her paranormal action/romance trilogy. Follow her adventures with her grandchildren and her ghost-hunting friends, as well as her ongoing flash fiction series at gilbertcuriosities.blogspot.com.

Godshalk, Barbara. "Yard Sale," "Driving Lessons"
Barbara is a full time mommy and writer of memoir pieces living in Mickleton, New Jersey with her amazing husband. She studies martial arts and bakes in the hopes of one day breaking even. Her daughter was born in 2008 and has taken over her house and much of her writing. Her pieces have been read on the Lime Channel of Sirius Satellite radio and published on the website www.inthepowderroom.com.

Harden, Bill. "The Junkyard"
Bill Harden is a lifelong resident of South Jersey. He is a new writer who is recently exploring writing opportunities. His interests include fiction and history. This is his first publication.

Hardy, Christine L. "Radiance," "The Gargoyle Cat"
Christine Hardy can't stop writing no matter how hard she tries. She writes mainstream fiction, poetry and epic fantasy. She can be found on Facebook as Christine L. Hardy, and her website is: www.ChristineLHardy.com.

Hollinger, Amy. "Hole in the Sky"
A South Jersey native, Amy has been a member of the South Jersey Writers' Group since 2006. She is an administrator by trade, and usually writes young adult fiction. One day, she hopes to actually complete a full manuscript. She blogs sporadically at: www.thegetoutgirl.com, and tweets voraciously @thegetoutgirl.

Knipp, James. "No Fun Joe"
Jim lives in South Jersey with a very patient wife and three teenage daughters who never fail to amaze and frustrate him, often at the same time. He has written several short stories and is currently working on a novel. Jim's somewhat skewed view of the universe can be found online at knippknopp.wordpress.com.

Magrowski, K.A. "Apparitions of Murder"
K.A. Magrowski is a South Jersey-based writer hoping to secure a book deal before the zombie apocalypse or an alien invasion, whichever happens first. She can be found on social media (and World of Warcraft) usually when she should be writing. Her website is kamagrowski.wordpress.com.

Szajner, Shelley. "The Feathered Messenger"
Shelley is an author, essayist, and illustrator who works as a graphic designer for a small book publisher. She earned a BA in Illustration from Rowan University and is currently working on the middle grade fantasy novel, *Oghalon.* You can follow Shelley's adventures as a writer at www.shelleyszajner.com.

Zamora-Mackay, Mieke. "The Walk"
Mieke is a wife and mother of two kids who are growing up faster than she could have imagined. She works full-time as a paralegal and writes women's romance, young adult and middle grade fiction. Follow her journey into the world of writing and reading on her blog, The Author-In-Training, at www.miekezmackay.com and on Twitter @MZMackay.

15900820R00087

Made in the USA
Charleston, SC
26 November 2012